*A
Harlequin
Romance*

OTHER
*Harlequin Romances*
by ISOBEL CHACE

# THE WEALTH OF THE ISLANDS

by

ISOBEL CHACE

HARLEQUIN BOOKS

TORONTO
WINNIPEG

Original hard cover edition published in 1971
by Mills & Boon Limited, 17-19 Foley Street,
London   W1A 1DR, England

© Isobel Chace 1971

Harlequin edition published September, 1972

SBN 373-01618-2

Printed in Canada

For
George and Mary la Frenais

# CHAPTER ONE

HELEN'S first sight of the Islands was from the aeroplane that had brought her from New Zealand, hopping from one group of islands to the next right across the Pacific Ocean. They spread out beneath her in the shape of a rather battered horseshoe with a long coral reef practically enclosing the open end. Through the gap, boats of varying sizes came and went, some of them transporting goods from one island to another, others setting out on the longer voyage to Fiji or Samoa, or even to the New Hebrides.

"Pretty, ain't it?" the pilot remarked laconically.

Pretty was an understatement, Helen thought. The Islands were the most delicious shade of green, edged with silver-white sands and set in a very blue sea. Even from a height she could see the palm trees waving gently in the soft breeze, their heads nodding towards each other in a slow, stately dance.

"I'm going down," the pilot said suddenly. "You can see the landing strip jutting out into the sea over there. There wasn't an island big enough in Melonga to take an airstrip. Before the war, you had to come by boat or not at all, but they made this soon enough when the Japs were coming." He grinned, enjoying her reaction of dismay as she saw what he meant by airstrip. From the sky it looked more like a fragile jetty protruding out into a shallow green coloured bay.

"Is it long enough?" she asked huskily.

His grin grew broader. "I'll set you down all right," he promised.

Even so, she shut her eyes tight as they swooped

7

down towards the island and only opened them when she felt the wheels of the aircraft lurch on to a solid surface and knew that they were safely down.

"Feel better?" the pilot asked unsympathetically.

"More or less," she agreed. And then she laughed. "Is there anything else on this island except the airstrip?" she wondered.

"Not much." He shrugged his shoulders. "The hotel is on the main island. There'll be a boat along some time to take you there, I dare say."

"And what will you do?" As far as she could see there was nothing on the island at all except a collection of huts and a fringe of palm trees that were growing, tall and straggly, round the inland end of the strip.

"I'll be getting on." He smiled across at her, his eyes unbelievably blue. "But I'll be back to see you some time, don't you worry about that! Shall I find you at the hotel?"

Helen nodded doubtfully. "I'll leave you my address there whatever I do," she promised. She twisted the wedding-ring on her finger nervously. "That is," she added, "if I stay at all."

"Oh, you'll stay! They won't let you get away!" he comforted her cheerfully. "A pretty girl like you can be sure of a welcome anywhere!"

"Even with Gregory de Vaux?" she queried bitterly.

"Can't say I know the man personally," the pilot said. "But I guess he's human like the rest of us!"

Helen smiled at him gratefully. "Did you know Michael?" she asked him next.

"Who else do you suppose flew him out here?" the pilot retorted. "Look, if you'll take a word of advice from me, you won't worry so. You get yourself fixed up and I'll fly your sister-in-law in to you next time I come. With the two of you together, you can hardly get into much trouble, can you?"

Helen's spirits recovered enough to enable her to giggle. "Heaven knows," she said, "we've led a pretty respectable life this last year!"

"Well, there you are then!" He pulled off his flying gear and opened the door in the main cabin of the plane for her to alight. "You'll find the Customs in one of those sheds," he told her. "They'll see you right. 'Bye now, Helen, it's been a joy to have you on board!"

She shook hands with him, thinking how odd it was that on this side of the world one never rated a surname. No one had called her Mrs. Hastings since she had arrived in New Zealand. It was Helen all the time, even from people she had never met before and never would again.

"Good luck!" the pilot called after her as she clambered down the steps and began to walk across the strip of concrete towards the shacks on the other side.

"Thanks," she called back. "And thanks for flying me out!"

He made a gesture in the air, signifying his approval. "It was great!" he assured her. "Made a change from the normal freight I bring here, I can tell you!"

Helen hesitated, wondering if she should ask him to treat her sister-in-law gently. Poor Anita, who had never flown anywhere in her whole life. But she thought better of it, waved her hand in a friendly salute and turned her face towards the Islands and the formalities of arrival there.

Michael Hastings had been a peculiarly handsome young man. The first time Helen had seen him she had been completely bowled over by his bright blue eyes, so curiously like the pilot's she had just left, and his floppy fair hair that was always in his eyes. It had only been a matter of time before she had thought she was in love with him, and hardly any time after that she had been sure of it.

They had met on a wild holiday scheme, organised by a group of students, that had gone diving off the coast of Ireland, hoping to find the wreck of one of the ships of the Spanish Armada, long rumoured to have come to grief somewhere in the vicinity. They hadn't found much, but she and Michael had been far too busy discovering one another to care.

"What brought you on such a holiday?" he had asked her.

"I enjoy it," she had answered. She had been too shy to tell him that diving had long been the major passion of her life. She was good at it too, and had spent most of her holidays helping out with one expedition or another. Because she was a teacher she had long holidays and she had made the most of them. "What are you doing here?" she had asked him in her turn.

He had grinned at her. "Bird-spotting!" he had told her frankly.

They had been inseparable after that. Sometimes Helen had been aware of an impatience within her when she had watched Michael dive with the others. She was a perfectionist about these things, she admitted that, but even so she hadn't been able to approve of Michael's exuberant technique, or of the risks he took. He in his turn had laughed at her safety precautions and had accused her of cowardice. "It's forgivable in a woman," he had added, "but it wouldn't be in a man!" And for some reason neither of them had fully understood, they had collapsed into helpless laughter.

A few weeks later they had been married. The service had been a terrifying ordeal, dominated for Helen by the presence of Michael's mother, who was the most terrible and forbidding person she had ever met. In a way, Helen had thought afterwards, it hadn't been her wedding at all. Mrs. Hastings, senior, had made that devastatingly clear. It had been *Michael's* wedding, his mother had made quite sure of that. Even the guests had been greeted by Michael and his mother, with Michael's sister, Anita, trailing along behind, her cheeks pale and her eyes anxious.

That had been the cause of their first quarrel. It had been a rather one-sided quarrel, with her throwing all the hurtful words she could think of and Michael remaining maddeningly calm and forgiving. One grew used to Mother, had been his favourite slogan. Only Helen had never grown used to his mother and knew even then that she never would.

And then three weeks later, while she had still been in the gorgeous golden glow of a thoroughly successful honeymoon, Michael had broken the news to her that he was off to the other side of the world. He had decided to go diving in the Melonga Islands for gold.

"It was my father's ship, you know," he had told her proudly. "He was sent by the Navy to pick up the Islands' gold just before the Japanese swept across the Pacific in the last war. The ship ran against a hidden coral reef and sank without trace. But there's a chap who's going to get the gold out. He's working for the Melongan Government. There's an advertisement in today's paper for divers. I'm going to apply."

At first Helen hadn't objected very strenuously. She had looked up the Islands in an atlas and had found them at last, a sprinkling of dots lost amidst the bright blue of the Pacific.

"When do we leave?" she had asked. "I can't wait to dive in the Pacific. My father always said it was the best place in the world!"

Michael had looked put out and quite sulky. "That's the point," he had said at last. "You don't leave. You're going to stay with Mother and Anita until I get back. I've arranged it all with Mother. She says there isn't any point in paying rent for this place just for one, and I agree with her. I'm sorry, darling, but that's the way it has to be! This chap doesn't go for women mucking up the expedition anyway!"

She had argued, of course. She had said some pretty bitter things which she knew she would regret for the rest of her life. But it had all been to no avail. She might just as well have saved her breath. Michael had gathered his gear together with a good humour that appeared not to even notice her objections to being left in such a fashion. Helen had never come across such tactics before, and long before he actually left, she had had to admit that she had lost the battle on all fronts. She had even been forced to agree that she would stay with his mother and Anita while he was away, though she knew that she would hate every minute of it—and so would her mother-in-law.

For three months she had existed rather than lived in the strained atmosphere that the Hastings called family life. Then a telegram had come from Melonga, addressed simply to Mrs. Hastings. Her mother-in-law had opened it with an expressionless face. When she had read it, she had folded it carefully, and put it away in her pocket.

"Michael is dead," she had said to Helen, and then she had calmly and deliberately walked out of the room.

"Welcome to Melonga!" The freshly painted sign was the only sign of life that Helen could see at the first of the shacks by the airstrip. She walked on past it towards the second, a newer building, that someone had taken the trouble to re-thatch recently.

"Is anyone there?" she called out.

"You off dat plane?" the reply came lazily. "Come in, now. Where's you for? The hotel?"

Helen crouched down to get in the door and blinked rapidly to accustom her eyes to the dark interior. A Polynesian man was sitting, cross-legged, on the floor. He rose slowly to his feet at the sight of her, a great smile breaking over his face.

"How come you come here on the freight plane?" he asked her admiringly.

"There didn't seem to be any other way to come," Helen answered dryly.

"Oh, there is !" the man claimed. "There's a boat every month and an American flight here now too. That's because of the hotel. Have you seen an American hotel?" he asked with ill-concealed awe. "It's the biggest building on the Islands. Mr. Harmon says, come the season, we're going to be swamped by all the American visitors that will come to his hotel. He's arranging transport just as fast as he can."

Helen looked bewildered. "I see," she said. "And how do I get to this hotel?"

"It's on the main island." The man nodded slowly. "First of all, I check your papers." He laughed softly. "People landing here ! I check freight all the time ! This the first time I check a young lady !"

Apparently he knew what to do, though. He stamped her passport with a neat symbol bearing the legend of Melonga Islands, and handed her documents back to her with a courtly bow.

"Is someone coming to meet you?" he asked when he had finished.

She shook her head. She was beginning to think that she would never get off this barren island. "How do you come and go?" she enquired.

"Government boat," he said. "But not allowed passengers. No trouble though. The *Sweet Promise* will come by soon. They'll give you a lift across the water."

"When are they due?" Helen asked rather desperately.

"Soon," he answered soothingly. "They come by soon."

Helen was glad to leave the hut and go outside

13

again. She looked anxiously at her watch and saw that it was already five o'clock in the evening. If this boat didn't come soon, it would be dark. She didn't much like the thought. It wasn't that she was afraid of the dark, but who knew what kind of a boat the one that was coming might be? She could see vividly in her mind's eye the fragile outrigger canoes that she knew most of the islanders used. How would she ever get her things on board such a thing? And she wasn't suitably dressed for such an adventure. She took a rueful look at her neat, tight skirt, and the ruffed blouse she was wearing, fastened with a cameo brooch at the neck. It suited her rather austere features and the way she wore her hair in a frankly Edwardian style, but it would not suit clambering in and out of any but the most civilised kind of transport.

The island she was on was not very large. In twenty minutes she had completely walked round its circumference. From one point, she had been able to see the whole chain of islands looping round the horseshoe-shaped lagoon. The main island was as big as all the others put together, but she could only just make it out in the distance. The islands spread for several miles, the work of how many million little creatures who had died and left their coral skeletons behind them, until the islands had appeared after many million years, and the birds had clothed them with vegetation. It had all happened thousands of years before the advent of man, but he too had probably arrived more by a matter of chance than anything else. The Polynesians had been fantastic sailors in their past. They had set out across the incredible distances of the Pacific with no more than the stars to guide them, and had populated the islands one by one, settling down on the different places they landed, and forgetting over the long generations their nautical past and the strength of purpose that had taken them so many, many thousands of miles.

Helen scuffed her shoe in the white coral sand and watched the multitude of tiny crabs that covered the beach running for cover. She was so intent on what she was doing that she didn't notice the Polynesian official running across the sand towards her.

"The *Sweet Promise* is almost here," he told her. "I've hailed them to pull in and collect you. It's best that you go and stand at the end of the airstrip. The water is deep there and they can come in right alongside."

In fact it formed an almost perfect jetty. Helen stood there waiting for the boat to come in close, the gold of the sun catching her hair and giving a touch of its own glory to her skin. But she was unaware of this herself. She had only eyes for the sailing ship coming towards her, its red and white striped sails flapping idly in the evening stillness. She was an old boat, but in her time she had been a lady and her lines still bore witness to her nobler beginnings. Helen wondered what she was doing here now, and who owned such a boat and therefore the delight of slipping back and forth amongst the islands of the Pacific, subject to no one but their own needs.

"You like her?" the Polynesian asked with a grin.

"She's perfect!" Helen breathed. "A coat of paint and some less mended sails and she'd be beautiful!"

The Polynesian laughed. "The boss likes her the way she is!" he informed her. "The paint will have to wait until the end of his work here."

Helen was so intent on the boat that she couldn't have cared less about her owner. Sheer, naked envy stirred within her. How she would loved to have owned a boat like that. How her father would have done before her! It was ideal in every way—not so large as to need a whole crew to handle her, but big enough to be able to live on board and to use her as a base for diving, or for carrying a small amount of cargo, or even just to sail the oceans in a modicum of comfort.

*Sweet Promise* was a name to conjure with, for she did indeed promise a hundred sweet adventures for anyone lucky enough to have the handling of her.

Standing on the deck at the bows was a lean man in a filthy yachting cap.

"I suppose you want to go to the main island?" he greeted her as soon as he came within earshot. "How much luggage have you?"

"Not much," she answered.

The man hailed the Polynesian official and told him to throw her cases aboard on to the deck. "I'll stow it away in a second," he said lazily. "Do you think you can jump aboard?" he added to Helen, eyeing her straight skirt with a half-doubtful, half-mischievous look.

"I can try," she assured him.

He grinned. "Don't bother!" he said. "I'll come ashore for you!"

He was as good as his word. Sun-tanned bare feet landed with a thud beside her and his strong hands had grasped her under her elbows and had manhandled her aboard long before she had time to open her mouth to protest.

"We can't allow you to get your finery wet," he laughed at her. "You'll want to arrive at the hotel looking as fresh as you do right now. Am I wrong?"

Helen didn't answer him. She rubbed her elbows, trying not to feel foolish. The scrubbed decks of the boat swayed beneath her and she had to clutch on to the hand-rail to keep her balance. There was a smell of diesel oil mixed with salt and canvas that she remembered so well from other boats in other times.

"Oh, you are lucky!" she exclaimed.

His eyes met hers, sharp with interest. "So you've been aboard boats before," he said. "But not in these parts, I fancy?"

Helen shook her head. "In Europe," she said. "Mostly with my father," she added. "I haven't done much sailing of late."

His eyes went straight to her wedding-ring and then back to her face. "That's the penalty of marrying," he said abruptly.

"It need not be," she answered.

He hurried away in his bare feet to the rear of the boat and shoved the engine into gear and set their course for straight out to sea, avoiding the hidden reefs as he made his way towards the harbour and small port on the main island. Helen waved to the Polynesian Customs man and he waved vigorously back at her, glad to see his protégée successfully on her way. How lovely it was, Helen thought, as the water slapped playfully against the bow and the wind caught in her hair, giving her a taste of the freedom that only boats and a wide sea to sail in can give.

She sat on the roof of the cabin, her feet stretched out before her to keep her balance, and watched the men working on the boat around her. Most of the crew were Polynesians, their brown bodies gleaming in the evening light. They were all of them big men, their flesh as soft as a woman's, deceiving the eye, because underneath their muscles were iron strong.

A few minutes later the man was back beside her. "You'd be safer in the saloon," he said abruptly. "Come on in and I'll make you some coffee."

She thanked him and, although she was sorry to leave her vantage point on deck, she followed him down the narrow companionway into the saloon. It was bigger than she had expected it to be. Lined in polished wood, it was still possible to sit on the seats that lined the central space and see out through the oval portholes.

"You have a beautiful boat!" Helen told him with appreciation. "How long have you had her?"

"Some years," he replied cautiously. He plonked some instant coffee into the bottom of two mugs and poured boiling water on the top. "Milk?" he asked.

She nodded and accepted the steaming mug he held

17

out to her. The coffee was very strong and bitter, but it was good and very refreshing.

"I needed that!" she said with appreciation, and smiled up at him.

"Where are you from?" he asked her.

"Today?"

"Yes, today, if you like."

"I was flown out with the freight for the Islands from New Zealand." She yawned apologetically. "It was a very early start!" she confessed.

He grinned. "You look none the worse for it," he complimented her.

She blushed faintly, aware suddenly of how closely he had been looking at her. "Thank you," she said quietly. "My name is Hastings, Mrs. Helen Hastings."

His face hardened dramatically. "Indeed?" he said coldly. "Then why have you come here, Mrs. Hastings? You should have known that there would be nothing here for you."

Helen twisted her fingers together to give herself courage. "I thought I could carry on where Michael left off," she explained awkwardly.

He stood up. "Wouldn't it have been wiser to have written first?" he suggested with icy politeness.

"I don't see that it's any of your business!" Helen retorted. "It's between me and Gregory de Vaux. There's no reason why he shouldn't employ me—I'm a much better diver than Michael ever was!"

"You'd need to be!" he snorted. "And I can assure you that Gregory de Vaux has never been known to employ a woman!"

"There can always be a first time!" she shot back at him.

"But not with you!" he snapped.

"Why not?" she insisted.

"Because," he said, and he sounded as if he enjoyed saying it, "I am Gregory de Vaux!"

There was a moment's silence. Helen looked at him

with wide eyes. Of course, she thought, that was what he was doing with the boat. But he didn't look like a man entrusted with such a mission. She glanced down at his bare feet and the torn bottom of his trousers. Why, he could even do with a shave! And goodness knew when he had last had his hair cut! And yet she had to admit that the boat was spotless and the equipment well looked after. It was a puzzle to her to know what to make of him.

"But you don't understand," she said. "I have Anita, my sister-in-law, to consider. I *made* her come with me. I had to. You don't know what it's like living with Michael's mother."

"I can imagine," he admitted with a fleeting smile. "But I don't quite see what it has got to do with me. I can't run my whole business round Michael's relatives, you know."

She held her head up high and looked him squarely in the eyes. "I'm not suggesting that you should!" she said carefully. "I'm only suggesting that you are short of divers—you were before Michael—before Michael died—and therefore you *need* me, just as much as I need a job!"

He looked at her with a certain sympathy. "But I don't employ women," he told her. "The men get upset and the whole expedition falls apart. I've had it happen to me before!"

Helen bit her lip. "I don't think you understand," she said desperately. "I have to dive for you! And as for my being a woman, Michael isn't so long dead that I shall be looking for any romantic adventures. I can assure you of that!"

He laughed at that! With his head thrown back and with his hands on his hips, he looked more like a pirate than ever.

"You underrate yourself!" he told her frankly.

Helen drank her coffee uncomfortably. "Well, you needn't be so beastly about it!" she commented.

He stopped laughing and leaned his brown, surprisingly well-kept hands on the table in front of him. "I'm sorry," he said sincerely. "I didn't mean to be beastly. I'll tell you what I'll do. I'll give you a trial run some time and you can show me what you can do. But I'm not promising anything! Is that quite clear?"

It was clear enough, she thought. He would allow her to dive just to please her, and then he would tell her that she was not suitable for the work he was doing. Still, it was a beginning. She knew she was a highly competent diver and she had no doubts at all that she would be able to prove her worth to him. She sat back in her seat and smiled.

"All right," she said. "That's fair enough."

She could tell that he was taken back by her confidence, but he shrugged the matter off and glanced down at his watch. "We'll be at the main island in about half an hour," he told her. "Is anyone expecting you?"

"They know I'm coming some time, but I didn't know that I'd be here today. A friend of my father's, a Miss Corrigan, has arranged a room for me and for my sister-in-law when she comes, at the hotel."

Gregory de Vaux stared at her. "Miss Corrigan?" he exclaimed. "Oh no! Don't tell me you know her! The old gorgon has only got to take to you and she'll twist me round her little finger—"

"Are you afraid of her, Mr. de Vaux?" Helen asked gently.

He glared at her. "Certainly not! Only I want to make up my own mind about your worth as a diver!"

Helen chuckled. "And so you shall," she assured him soothingly.

"You don't know Miss Corrigan!" he groaned.

Helen laughed again. "I am sure I shall like her very much indeed," she said.

"I can believe it! Well, since fate is conspiring against me, I'm glad it's such a pretty fate!" He disappeared up the companionway, his bare feet slapping against the lino-covered stairs. It was strange how much she noticed his going. His presence was rather like lightning, devastating, but noticeably exciting. She would enjoy working for him, she thought. It would make a pleasant change from mourning her dead husband in the suffocating atmosphere of her mother-in-law's house. She and Anita would have time to learn to live again and that, at the moment, was all she asked of life. Particularly for Anita, her tired, pale, and rather insignificant sister-in-law.

# CHAPTER TWO

ANITA had been Helen's main worry after Michael had died. She had not noticed at first what Mrs. Hastings' grief was doing to her daughter, for it had been bad enough living in the Hastings house when Michael had been alive, and Helen had moved out as soon as possible after the news had come that he was dead.

At first they had all been surprised how well Michael's mother was taking the news. She had derived a strange pleasure from the fact that the telegram announcing the death had been delivered to her instead of to Helen. Later, when the confirming letter had come, she had snatched that away too, and it had been days before she had allowed Helen to read it.

"It's addressed to me!" she had said defiantly. "I am Mrs. Hastings!"

"So, unfortunately, am I!" Helen had answered.

"So you're regretting it," Mrs. Hastings had accused her with satisfaction. "I knew that you never really cared for Michael."

Helen wished that she had known it too. But she was too proud to show her sorrow to her in-laws. Any tears that she shed, she shed when she was alone, in the privacy of her own room. And then, when it had become too unbearable to go on living in the same house as Michael's mother, she had left and had found a room for herself in London, fairly near the school where she was still teaching.

In fact, so busy had she been coping with her own grief that it had been some weeks before she had noticed the change in Anita. She was ashamed to

22

admit that she had done little enough to befriend Anita in the past. The girl had seemed little more than a pale shadow of her mother, following after her wherever she went, fetching and carrying for her and generally making herself useful, with no friends of her own, and apparently very little desire to live a life of her own. Helen had been all the more shocked therefore when, out of a sense of duty she had visited her mother-in-law to discuss the terms of Michael's will. Anita's face had fallen away into shadowed, tightly drawn skin stretched over bones, and her eyes were little more than two pools of sheer misery.

"Anita, what's the matter?" Helen had greeted her.

"Ssh!" Anita had warned her. "Mother is listening."

Helen had stood in the front doorway and had frowned at the pale, fair girl before her. "Why don't you ever stand up for yourself?" she had asked her irritably.

Anita had sighed. "You don't understand," she had whispered.

"Oh yes, I do!" Helen had snapped back. "I understand a great deal too well! But if you let it go on you'll spend the rest of your life being nobody but *poor little Anita*! Is that what you want?"

Anita had winced. "Perhaps that's what I am," she had said.

"Rubbish!" Helen had said, much as she would have done to a tiresome child at the school where she taught. "Where is the old witch? I'll soon fix her!"

"Oh, but you mustn't!" Anita had pleaded. "She's so unhappy about Michael. She keeps on and on—"

"And I suppose his death meant nothing at all to you?" Helen had asked her witheringly. "Or to me either, come to that!" she had added with a touch of bitterness that was normally quite foreign to her nature. "You'd better leave me to see Mrs. Hastings alone," she had told Anita imperiously. "Go and make some tea or something, and for heaven's sake put on some make-up. You look like a little ghost!"

Mrs. Hastings had not been an easy proposition. She had, apparently, taken it upon herself to go into Michael's financial affairs, and it seemed that he had left virtually nothing. "So you see," she had told Helen with ill-concealed triumph, "he's left you almost penniless!"

Helen had said nothing at first, then finally she had burst out with, "Mrs. Hastings, I have quite a bit of money saved. I'm going out to the Melonga Islands myself to find out what really happened to Michael, and I want Anita to come with me."

"It's out of the question!" Mrs. Hastings had gasped. "What should I do without her?"

"I'm more worried about Anita," Helen had observed dryly. "Have you looked at her recently?"

It had been a long battle before Michael's mother had given way. She had refused to pay so much as a penny towards Anita's fare to New Zealand and had made the poor girl's life quite miserable before they had finally left, but leave they had on the long exhausting flight right round the world to New Zealand. Yet, despite the tiring, non-stop flying, the eating of meals at unheard-of hours, and the hours of sleep snatched here and there at curious times, Anita had looked a great deal better on arrival than she had when they had left.

Twenty-four hours after their arrival in Auckland, Anita had gone down with appendicitis, and so it was that Helen had come on to the Melonga Islands alone. And now, she thought with satisfaction, she had got the chance of getting the job she wanted, the job that was going to keep them while they were there. There was the sound of shouting on the deck above her head and she flew up the companionway to see what was happening. The last light of the sun lit the small harbour and the island beyond, silhouetting the palm trees that fringed the silver sands. She had finally arrived.

The jetty had been built from roughly felled trees, joined together to form a platform, alongside which the boats of the local inhabitants could be tied up in safety. It was a rickety structure, but it served its purpose and so no one had ever thought of changing it for something more elaborate.

The *Sweet Promise* slipped into the still waters of the little harbour and berthed easily alongside the jetty.

"Now all we have to do is get you ashore!" Gregory de Vaux said teasingly.

Helen smiled. "I didn't know I was going boating," she said.

"No?" He lifted his eyebrows faintly and grinned at her. "If it weren't for the wedding-ring on your finger, I'd think you were too young for such adventures."

"It doesn't mean that I'm inefficient—at diving, I mean," she said defensively.

He looked amused. "Of course not," he agreed. "We'll be able to find out about that tomorrow. Meanwhile, I'll take you to the hotel and book you in there."

She thanked him prettily, uneasily aware that he was adept at making her feel feminine and useless in a way that Michael had never been able to. She wished he wouldn't stand there, looking as if he didn't care a damn about anything, with the last of the light bronzing his skin until he looked like a statue of some pagan god demanding someone's worship. Well, it wouldn't be hers, she told herself with a no-nonsense little nod of the head. She was far too worldly wise to be taken in by a handsome face and a light-hearted manner.

Even so, she was not prepared to allow him to hand

her ashore. "I can manage perfectly well by myself!" she assured him sternly.

"All right," he drawled. He leaned back against the masthead and watched her struggle with her luggage. When she dropped one of the suitcases on the deck, he signalled with a lazy finger for one of the Polynesian crew to take it from her and carry it ashore, but he made no move himself. He only watched her until she was nervous and convinced that she would do something daft, just because he had succeeded in unsettling her.

"Are you sure you can manage the jump?" he drawled as she hesitated before taking off to land on the flimsy jetty, some feet below.

"Of course I'm sure!" she answered exasperatedly.

"Pride goes before a fall," he commented, as though he were speaking to himself.

*That* made her jump! She took off with her eyes tight shut and landed with a jerk that knocked all the breath out of her. The timbers of the jetty creaked ominously, but to her infinite relief they held beneath her, and she gazed triumphantly upwards at the mocking face of Gregory de Vaux.

"See!" she said.

He laughed and the Polynesian crew laughed with him, their dark faces breaking into wide grins and their heavy flesh jumping up and down in time to the great guffaws of laughter that came out of their mouths. Helen was at first startled and then she began to laugh herself.

"What's so funny?" she demanded.

"You are!" Gregory told her. He jumped down beside her as agile as a cat and grabbed her suitcases in either hand. "Come on," he said. "Let's get you checked in and settled."

He was as good as his word. He led the way through the shanty town and fish market that had grown up round the harbour, to the wider streets beyond, lined by utilitarian houses, mostly built on a single-storey plan, past the Government buildings, and finally to the hotel itself. It must have been by far the biggest building on the islands. It towered some twenty storeys in the air, a vast construction of steel and glass in symmetric patterns of windows and balconies.

"Is *this* the hotel?" Helen asked with awe.

"That's right," Gregory de Vaux assured her cheerfully. He looked the building up and down with an amused smile. "Ain't it somethin'?" he said.

It appeared that he was not at all in awe of the place. He opened the heavy glass doors for her to go into the foyer first, and came in after her, burying his naked toes into the deep pile of the carpet.

"Gregory!" a strident female voice reproved him.

"Why, Ethel," he drawled. "I have your young friend from England here. I gather you are expecting her?"

An English lady of uncertain age came out from behind the desk, her hotel-key chinking in an eager, trembling hand. "Where is she?" she screamed in acute pleasure. "I've been *longing* for her to arrive! I knew her father, you know. Such a *kind* man!" She advanced across the foyer, her cheeks and dewlap flapping, her pale grey eyes alight with interest and delight. "My dear!" she exclaimed, embracing Helen with an awkwardness that betrayed her lack of practice. "My dear! How like your father you are!"

"I'm surprised that you can see what she's like in this gloomy place," Gregory observed flatly.

Miss Corrigan shook her head at him. "You are a naughty boy!" she informed him roundly. "Helen has come here as *my* guest, so you can just mind your own business!"

Gregory grinned. "I can't very well do that," he said. "She's already asked me for a job."

Miss Corrigan shuddered visibly. "And are you going to give her one?"

Gregory shrugged his shoulders. "It depends how good she is," he said cagily.

"There's no doubt about that," Miss Corrigan said roundly, her cheeks quivering with emotion. "She was taught by her *father*!"

Gregory's face became serious for an instant. "I don't care who taught her! I'm not having any more amateurs botching up my operations and that's that! Nor am I having any more conflict with the authorities about unnecessary deaths, or anything at all—"

"Ssh, dear," Miss Corrigan interrupted him, shocked. "Michael was this girl's husband!"

Gregory looked at Helen, his face hardening. "So he was," he said at last. "I'd forgotten that."

He turned on his heel and walked quickly out of the hotel, the bottoms of his torn jeans flapping round his bare feet. Even from his back view it was possible to tell how close his suppressed anger was to erupting like a geyser all round them. "I'll call for you in the morning," he said from the entrance, and added by way of an afterthought, "And wear something sensible, will you?"

Helen watched his departure, her eyes wide with indignation. "And just who does he think he is?" she demanded.

Miss Corrigan shook her head sadly. "He's a fine boy really," she said pacifically. Her eyes met Helen's, steely grey and twinkling. "It's a pity, dear, you're any connection of Michael's—"

"I'm not just a connection, I'm his *widow*!" Helen pointed out.

"Yes, dear, I know. Very sad. I *feel* for you. I'm sure Gregory does too underneath. Only Michael's death was a teeny bit inconvenient, if you don't mind my saying so. Everything was held up for so *long* while they held endless investigations that got absolutely nowhere. So you can't be surprised if Gregory prefers to forget all about him, can you?"

"Yes," said Helen loudly, "I can. I'm sorry he was inconvenienced, but Michael *died*. Doesn't anyone care about that?"

Miss Corrigan patted her hand with awkward sympathy. "You do, it would seem," she observed dryly. "You can't expect the rest of us to be so involved emotionally, my dear. Michael was a loner all the time he was here. None of us really knew him at all well."

"Nevertheless, he was a man and he died," Helen insisted, swallowing a painful lump in her throat.

"Quite right, my dear," Miss Corrigan agreed. "But although one mourns the dead, life *does* go on. You'll find that out. Now, I must find young Peter Harmon and he can take you to your room. You'll dine with me tonight, of course?"

Helen licked her lips. "Thank you very much," she said.

"Then I'll find Peter," Miss Corrigan said again, and she rushed off into the interior of the hotel, her head several inches in front of her feet in her anxiety to arrive at her destination faster than she could actually travel. Later, Helen was always to think of it as the one outstanding characteristic of Miss Ethel Corrigan. Her interest took her everywhere and she never had enough time to do all that she wanted to, so she was perpetually in a hurry, swooping from one place to another, her head stuck well out ahead of her and with her cheeks quivering with enthusiasm for whatever had seized her fancy at that particular moment. Miss Corrigan had lived for so long on the Islands that they had become her whole life, but she had by no means restricted her mental horizons. Anything and everything was grist to her mill as she poked about the place she had made her own particular domain.

Helen lingered in the foyer, studying the photographs of the Islands which surrounded the wood-panelled walls, until a nervous, fair young man came to rescue her. He stood playing with his fingers, while she finished her tour of inspection. Then he cleared his throat noisily to attract her attention.

"Mrs. Hastings? Miss Corrigan said you had arrived. I'm the manager of the hotel."

Helen smiled at him. "Mr. Harmon?"

He looked taken aback. "Oh, you know my name? Miss Corrigan, I suppose," he added with a shy smile. "I'm pretty new here still," he confessed. "They only just finished building the hotel."

"But you are open?" Helen asked him anxiously.

"Oh yes," he agreed enthusiastically. "Actually our only customer so far is Miss Corrigan. She's decided she'd be more comfortable living with us. But pretty soon we're going to be right on the tourist map! Yes, ma'am! We're aiming pretty high here!"

Helen wondered how all the expected tourists were going to be brought to the Islands. As far as she knew there was only the one steamer a month which called at the tiny harbour. That, and the freight plane which had brought her in that evening. It seemed a far cry from American package tours coming and going in weekly shifts.

"I've given you a room at the top, as Miss Corrigan directed," Mr. Harmon went on. "For there you can get a view right over the bay. You can even see the different coloured corals of the reef. It's pretty beautiful!"

They went up in a lift that creaked with newness and walked a short way along a wide corridor before Mr. Harmon stopped outside one of the doors and opened it with the key he had brought with him. "Here we are!" he said in a pleased voice, and waited eagerly for her reaction.

He certainly had something to be pleased about. The room was full of flowers, beautifully arranged to lead the eye out on to the balcony and the sea beyond. It was too late to see the view properly now, but the lights from the boats twinkled across the moonlit scene, giving some faint idea of what it would be like in the morning light, with the sun shining from morn to night. The headboard of the bed was designed to resemble the spread tail of a paradise bird, and there was a chair to match set in the corner opposite. It was, Helen thought, rather overwhelming in its opulence.

"Goodness!" she exclaimed.

Peter Harmon laughed. "I have the next room ready for your sister-in law when she comes," he told her. "It's just the same."

Helen walked out on to the balcony and took a deep breath of air. "I never thought of the Pacific as *smelling*," she said, amused by her own fancy. "But it does, doesn't it? It's quite different from the Atlantic."

"I'll say!" Peter Harmon agreed. "And I ought to know. I haven't been here long myself. It's my first job as a full-blown manager, though I've always worked for the same group of hotels."

"Do you like it?" Helen asked him curiously.

He nodded vigorously. "It's fun seeing people enjoy themselves," he said. "Not the fancy types who are always around, but the people who have saved to have a really good bust! I like to see them eating good food and getting good service for their money. They've earned it, I reckon."

Helen found herself liking this fair American very much indeed. "I've never thought about it," she admitted. "I've hardly ever stayed in a hotel. When I was a child, we always went everywhere by boat and then I grew up and became a teacher."

His eyes bulged with astonishment. "A *teacher*? I thought you were going to be one of Gregory's divers. I thought you looked a sight too smart for that!"

Helen coloured faintly. "Too smart?"

Peter Harmon tugged nervously at his neatly tied tie. "Have you met Gregory yet?" he asked in hushed tones.

"Yes, I have," Helen said.

"Oh well," he said, completely embarrassed. "But he's always like that. I mean—"

"His boat is well kept, though," Helen observed.

"That's exactly what I mean!" Peter said with relief. "He isn't the tuxedo type. And you can say that again!"

Helen sighed. He wasn't any type that she had ever met, she thought to herself. But she was sure of one thing, he had enough sheer animal magnetism for a whole army of men, more in his little finger than this nice American had in his whole body. She puckered up her mouth and sighed again. She *disapproved* of any man being so attractive! Peter was right, he probably wasn't at all trustworthy. That might even have been why Michael had died. Goodness knows, he had been unnecessarily unkind about that! But she would have to kowtow to him long enough to get a job, but once the job was hers it would give her the very greatest pleasure to tell him just what she thought of him.

She shut the door after Peter had gone and went and stood on the balcony for a long time before she realised that she would be late if she didn't hurry up and change for dinner. Unpacking took her only a few minutes. She hung the dresses on hangers and put them away in the built-in wardrobe. The rest of her things she piled into drawers and left them to be sorted at her convenience later.

Miss Corrigan was waiting for her in the foyer when she went downstairs.

"I've made Peter serve dinner on the terrace," the old lady said as soon as she saw her. "It's prettier than the dining room, and anyway we don't want to eat in lonely state in that enormous place, do we?"

Helen agreed that they didn't. Besides, the balmy air of the evening appealed to her. They sat out on locally made cane chairs and sipped a fruit drink that was all the concession that Miss Corrigan was prepared to make to the cocktail hour.

"I disapprove of strong drink," she told Helen. "My father did so from conviction, I from habit. I am afraid you will have to humour me just this evening. Do you mind?"

Helen didn't mind at all. She accepted the drink that the waiter offered her and delighted in the sheer coolness of its icy contents. From somewhere in the distance, Polynesian songs were being sung, their tuneful quality coming across the still night air.

"What very pretty music!" Helen exclaimed.

Miss Corrigan's nose twitched with sudden and all-consuming interest. "Do you like it? It's my greatest passion in life! Unfortunately I can't sing a note myself and I have given up trying, but I go into the villages as often as I can to hear them singing their songs and telling of their legends. I take them down on tapes. I believe," she added in the humble tones experts are inclined to use when speaking of their own subject, "I believe that I have one of the largest collections of Polynesian music in the world. But then, of course, I have been here a long time to be able to acquire all the recordings that I have."

"Always in the Melonga Islands?" Helen asked her.

"Latterly," the old lady agreed. "Since before the war. I've got used to being here now and I don't want to move. The war did that to me. One couldn't move at all then and I got out of the way of wanting to."

"But weren't the Japanese here during the war?" Helen put in, fascinated by her hostess.

Miss Corrigan laughed. "Oh yes, we were occupied, you know. They sent an officer with about eight men here and they spent the duration of the war with us. I think they were rather sorry when it was all over and they had to go home. We had grown *quite* used to each other by that time. They had even managed to teach me Japanese—I think it made them less lonely to be addressed in their own language. Poor things, they came as stiff and starchy as you could wish, but life on the Islands soon changed all that!" she added with satisfaction.

Helen chuckled. She couldn't imagine even the Japanese getting the better of Miss Corrigan. "I believe you enjoyed it all!" she accused her.

Miss Corrigan looked thoroughly ashamed of herself. "I think I liked the excitement," she confessed. "It wasn't exciting for very long, but Japanese legends and customs are absolutely fascinating and the officer in charge of the party, Kitsimu-san, was really very knowledgeable about them. The hard part was at the end of the war when we all had to remember that we had been enemies. It is so out of the way here, we had practically forgotten." She sighed gustily. "But I want to hear about you, my dear. To *think* that you are Harold's daughter! Why, it seems just the other day that he married your mother! You're like him in your looks—"

"Am I?" Helen said lightly. "He always hoped I'd be like my mother. They were both killed in a car crash. You knew that, didn't you?"

Miss Corrigan creased up her forehead while she thought about it. "Yes," she said, "I did know, but I'd forgotten. I hope you didn't grieve, child. Harold wouldn't have liked it! And then there was that terrible affair with that young husband of yours!" She looked Helen straight in the eyes. "I do hope you are not a *sad* person?" she said accusingly.

Helen gave a startled gasp. "I—I don't think so," she said.

Miss Corrigan relaxed so violently that her chair creaked an ominous protest beneath her. "*That's* a relief! I must admit I did wonder when you wrote and said you were coming out here to take Michael's place with the expedition if you could. I suppose you were tired of teaching?"

"Not exactly," Helen tried to explain. "It was because of my sister-in-law, Anita. Michael's mother was driving her round the bend. I thought if I brought her out here, she would be far enough away to live her own life for a bit."

"Ah yes," Miss Corrigan nodded. "I had forgotten that she should have been with you. And are you expecting her to dive too?" she asked dryly.

Helen shook her head, laughing. "No, Anita would die sooner than put her head under water. I'm hoping to make enough while we're here to keep the two of us."

Miss Corrigan looked less than hopeful. "Gregory is so very *un*malleable, if you know what I mean," she warned gently.

Helen lifted her chin belligerently. "So am I. He can hardly deny me really," she added. "He badly needs another diver. He knows it and I know it."

"But after Michael dying like that, he doesn't want to employ a woman," Miss Corrigan explained earnestly. "Supposing you were to be killed too?"

Helen grinned, suddenly very sure of herself. "I'm a great deal better diver than Michael ever was! They won't kill me off so easily!"

Miss Corrigan laughed and then tried to look shocked. "Really, my dear," she protested. "What a thing to say! Do you think that Michael was deliberately killed?"

Helen shrugged. "I don't know," she said. "The only explanation of his death that we received was confused to say the least. That was another reason why I wanted to come here—to find out exactly what happened to Michael."

"You were in love with him?" Miss Corrigan asked, much as though the whole topic of love made her feel uncomfortable.

Helen said nothing for a long moment. "I think so," she said then.

"But you're not sure?" Miss Corrigan pursued her ruthlessly.

"No," Helen agreed, "I'm not sure. It seems so very long ago. We only had three weeks together and then he was gone. It's almost a year now since he died, and when I shut my eyes, I can't even see his face any more. All I can see is his mother—"

"And you would prefer not to?" Miss Corrigan added shrewdly.

Helen smiled sadly. "Yes, I would prefer not to," she agreed.

# CHAPTER THREE

IN the morning, Helen was still having breakfast when Gregory de Vaux arrived.

"Have some coffee?" she offered him, hastily finishing the piece of toast she was eating.

"Okay," he agreed. He poured himself some and heaped several spoonfuls of sugar into the cup. "What have you got in that bag?" he asked, kicking it with a bare foot.

"I always carry my own rubber suit," she answered. Didn't he ever wear any shoes, she wondered, or anything else but those torn jeans and a shirt that had seen better days?

"You won't need it here," he said tersely. "A swimming-suit is enough. The water stays pretty warm. The ship is jammed on to the reef, by the way. It isn't at all deep, thank goodness. At least it saves on the lights."

"How deep?" she countered, buttering another piece of toast because he didn't seem to be in such a hurry after all.

"About a hundred feet,"

Helen looked puzzled. "But how did Michael die, then?" she inquired. "I was sure in my own mind that he must have gone down too deep. I mean, I don't suppose you have a decompression chamber here?" She paused, studying his face. "Then it wasn't the bends?"

"I thought I'd explained in my letter," he said patiently. "Didn't you bother to read it?"

Helen winced away from the tone in his voice. It still hurt when she thought of the way her mother-in-law had whisked the letter away, not even allowing her a sight of it.

37

"Unfortunately," she said dryly, "it didn't appear to be addressed to me, so I never actually saw it."

"Well, for crying out loud! Who *do* you think it was addressed to?"

"Michael's mother," Helen answered with restraint, because she couldn't bear him to see how badly she had been hurt.

Gregory stared at her, open-mouthed. "You must have very strange customs in your family," he said at last. "But it isn't any of my business. Are you ready to go?"

She nodded and stood up, pushing her chair in under the table. Miss Corrigan had been right about the lonely state of the dining-room, she thought. It was too big for anyone to have to eat in it alone. And the palm tree that was the central feature of the decorations was a great mistake, for it towered up into the glass-domed roof and one couldn't even see it unless one craned one's neck to do so.

She grabbed her bag containing her rubber suit and hurried out after Gregory, a faint stirring of excitement within her as she thought of the clear blue water and how lovely it would be to feel it all round her. It was so long since she had been diving! Not since before her marriage. She shivered suddenly, remembering that that had been when she had met Michael. Oh well, she wouldn't dwell on it, she promised herself. She would think back to far happier days, when her father had been alive and they had dived together in the Mediterranean. With some success too, she remembered gratefully. But then her father had always been lucky in anything he had touched. They had teased him about it. Lucky in money *and* lucky in love, they had said with varying amounts of envy. Now, Helen had the money he had made and she wasn't lucky at all!

Gregory interrupted her reverie by pointing out the

copra plantations that fell away behind the little town that had grown up round the harbour.

"Before the war, they used to pay the Islanders in gold," he told her. "Now they have to accept paper like everyone else." He laughed. "There's a fortune down there in this ship, if we can ever get it out!"

"Why shouldn't we?" she responded gaily.

He looked at her with amusement. "The ship is pretty badly mauled," he warned her. "And that reminds me, look out for the coral. If you jag yourself on it, it takes a long, long time for the wounds to heal."

"I'll take care," Helen promised.

By day, the whole island looked different. She had thought she had known what to expect from films and pictures in geographical magazines, but the reality was more alive than any of these. True, it was dingier too, but she so very much preferred it. She particularly liked the older part of the town which they were walking through now: there was still the old tin-roofed trading post, now abandoned, and a whole series of houses in various stages of dilapidation, with thatched roofs and walls of woven palm leaves. Here and there, a new house shone pale green and gold amongst the dark browns and greys of the older homes, some of which had been long left to decay in their own time where they stood. Children peeked out through holes in the walls and came out laughing when they saw Gregory striding past. Dogs dashed hither and thither about their own business, but even they apparently thought it worth while to follow Gregory down to the rickety jetty. By the time they arrived there, Helen felt something of a Pied Piper, but Gregory showed no signs of even noticing the train of children at his heels.

He grinned when Helen, clad in shirt and slacks, jumped easily aboard the *Sweet Promise*, bag in hand, but he said nothing. He swung his own long body up over the bows and squatted down to check the diving equipment that he must have put there earlier.

"Look out, pidgins!" he shouted to the children, and they scattered away from the jetty, running for all they were worth. "Their parents will kill them if they interfere with my things," he added with a smile to Helen.

"They weren't doing any harm," Helen replied, her voice tinged with disapproval.

He laughed. "They talk big round here—bigger than their actions! Killing is only a light tanning, and most of the parents are too gentle even to think of doing that! You don't have to worry about the little beggars."

Helen was annoyed that he had seen through her so easily. "Where are the rest of the crew?" she asked to change the subject.

"Na-Tinn is just coming. His brother is down below, stowing some of the stuff away that we won't need today. His name is Taine-Mal."

Helen practised both names in her mind so that she wouldn't forget them and, at that very moment, one of the Polynesian sailors she had met the evening before came running along the jetty and leaped on board beside her.

"This is Na-Tinn," Gregory told her. Helen shook hands with the mountain of a man beside her. When he grinned at her, she saw that his teeth were hideously disfigured by being filed into points, giving him the expression of a shark rather than a man.

"Welcome on board," he said warmly.

Gregory came over to them and stood a few feet off with his hands on his hips. "She's Michael Hastings' wife," he drawled.

Na-Tinn withdrew his hand hastily. "That pidgin made life bad!" he said hoarsely, forgetting his precise English in the heat of the moment.

Helen's smile fell from her face and she turned away so that they would not be able to see the sudden tears which had rushed into her eyes. "I'm his widow, not his wife," she said huskily.

Na Tinn shook his head sadly. "Same thing," he muttered. "Why you come here?"

"Now that's a good question," Gregory agreed under his breath.

"Does it matter?" Helen said pugnaciously. "That's my business. As long as I can dive properly, I don't see that you need to know anything else!"

Gregory shrugged. "We'd better get going, then," he said. "Cast off, will you, Na-Tinn?"

Everybody had their own task once the boat was under way and Helen felt frankly in the way. As yet, no particular task had been assigned to her and she felt excluded, by Gregory and by the others, for something that was not her fault and which she didn't understand.

"Do you want to take a turn at the wheel?" Gregory asked her, when they were clear of the little harbour and its flotilla of fishing boats and canoes. It was uncanny the way he was able to read her thoughts! But on this occasion she didn't mind. She went aft as quickly as she could and squeezed into the cockpit beside him.

"May I really?" she asked eagerly.

"May as well see what use you're going to be on the boat as well as in the water," he grunted.

He took one hand away from the wheel, steering it casually with the fingers of one hand while she got herself into position. She had to get very close to him to put her own hands on the wheel at all and she was surprised by the hardness of his body and the disturbing quality of his warm breath on the back of her neck.

"Have you got it?" he asked her almost immediately.

"I think so," she said. It was hard to concentrate with him being so close to her, and that annoyed her. She had thought that she had long ago outgrown such adolescent reactions.

"Good," he said briefly, and was gone, a faint smile on his face, leaving her to steer the *Sweet Promise* out and away from the main island towards the reef where the Navy ship had come to grief so many years before.

It was a wonderful sensation to feel a deck under her feet again, to feel the lifting of the timbers straining against deep waters. She had forgotten how good it was, how much she loved the salt water on her face and the smell of the billowing canvas when the engine had been shut off, and the creaking sound of rope against tackle, augmented by the slapping of the boat's hull against the deep green waves.

Na-Tinn came and relieved her at the wheel after a while, when the wind had caught their sails and they were slipping through the sea with an easy lilt that delighted her.

"Taine-Mal will give you a cup of coffee if you go below," he told her with his wide, shark-faced grin. "Time to get ready to dive too. Boss, he say that !"

Helen was reluctant to give up the wheel that was tugging gently in her hands as if it were a living thing, but when he pointed ahead the water was so clear that she thought she could make out the tip of the reef they were aiming for and knew that it was indeed time for her to get ready for her first dive in the Pacific Ocean. She was nervous, but not abominably so. She was glad though of the hot coffee that Taine-Mal liberally supplied her with, grinning like his brother to show pointed teeth, all neatly filed in some terrible ceremony in his youth.

Gregory was already sitting on the edge of the deck with his feet dangling over the edge when she went back up on deck, her bathrobe pulled tightly about her. His body was burned gold in the sun and made hers seem whiter than it really was.

"Hi there!" he greeted her. "You've made it!" His smile was more friendly than she had expected.

"I do my best to please," she smiled back.

His eyes crinkled with sudden laughter. "You please all right," he said. "If you can only dive as well as you look, I'll take you on, I swear by Neptune and all the others that I will!"

Helen looked down her nose and frowned. "Do you know the legend of the boy and the dolphin?" she asked him.

"Only that it brings good luck," he admitted.

"My father once thought he saw a boy riding a dolphin," she said solemnly. "He was the luckiest man I've ever known. I was just wondering if there was any equivalent symbol of good luck for these waters."

He frowned. "If you're a good diver, you don't need good luck," he said smartly. "I should have thought you'd have known that?"

She nodded, not looking at him. "One always needs good luck," she said.

He didn't answer her. The sails came rushing down and hit the deck and Na-Tinn shouted to Gregory to drop the anchor.

"If he cuts it any finer, one of these days we'll end up on that reef ourselves!" Gregory swore to himself. He pulled the pin out of the anchor-chain and it dropped overboard in a clatter of metal links, gaining a firm purchase on the coral bank below them.

Helen stared over into the water, astonished at its clearness. It was quite easy to make out the rises and falls in the coral shelf and to watch the fish swimming in their shoals of fleeting colour, flashing to and fro up and down the reef in a constant search for food. She could even make out the lines of the sunken frigate that her father-in-law had once commanded. She shivered at the sight of it, already encrusted and looking quite unearthly under the fathoms of clear water that covered it and the valuable cargo that was somewhere still inside it. She could see where Gregory and, she supposed, Michael had torn back the welded metal in their efforts to gain an entrance, and she wondered why they had not forced a hatch, or even broken in the portholes. She would soon know, she thought, and took a deep breath to calm the nervous quiver of fear within her that came and went just as though she had never dived before.

Gregory fitted the compressed air cylinders to her back, but she tied her own leather belt around her waist, filling it with leaden weights to enable her to sink from the surface. If she were not careful, she would breathe too deeply, like any amateur, and need more weights to get her down, so she restricted the amount of air she took into her lungs with a calm desperation born of her urgency to succeed. For the first time it had come home to her that Gregory might not take her on, that she might fail to prove her worth to the expedition and that he would be only too pleased to turn her away because she was a woman and he didn't like employing women. When she shut her eyes, she had a clear vision of her mother-in-law's delight at her failure, and that steeled her determination as nothing else would have done.

"Ready?" Gregory asked her.

She nodded and he bent and adjusted the flippers on her feet and checked the meter on the breathing apparatus.

"Okay, you're go!" he said.

She took her mask in her hand, spat into it and washed it in the bucket of salt water that Na-Tinn held out to her. Carefully she adjusted it over her nose and eyes and then allowed herself to be lowered gently over the side in a kind of rope basket that Gregory had rigged up for that very purpose. The water was deliciously cool and she couldn't wait to be free to dive deep down into it. Above her, Gregory released the ropes and the basket fell away from her. She kicked out away from the *Sweet Promise*, then allowed herself to fall down and down until she was almost level with the coral shelf where the frigate lay and could see in intimate detail how the coral had been built up in the last few thousand years, the skeletons of more millions of tiny creatures than man could count, adding to one another and slowly forming a whole mountain beneath the sea to appear here and there as Pacific islands and the typical coral reefs that surrounded them.

Now that she was under water, Helen felt better. Her nervousness had gone. She wished she had prepared her mask with greater thoroughness, for it had misted slightly on the left-hand side. She had probably missed it when she had smeared it with saliva before rinsing it out, she thought, but it wasn't bad and she could see quite well enough for anything she wanted to do.

In all she must have allowed herself quite five minutes to acclimatise herself to her new surroundings. She kept remembering earlier dives she had made with her father and for an instant she longed for his comforting presence swirling through the waters towards her, just as he always had, releasing a fish straight into her face, or pulling one of the half dozen tricks he had never been able to resist. She was remembering the dive on which she had met Michael too. It was here that Michael had died, she thought in a sudden panic. Her skin prickled with fear, but then she looked upwards and saw the dark hull of the *Sweet Promise* above her and the panic subsided. What could go wrong? She wasn't one to

45

take stupid risks. She would approach the frigate only when she was ready to do so and when she could see her way clear to doing so. So why worry? Gregory couldn't make her take risks she didn't want to take!

She was ready then to go along the shelf to look at the frigate. She saw for the first time how she had fallen away from her original position on to her side, exposing the large, gaping hole where she had battered herself against the reef, causing her to sink. The edges of the hole were too jagged for it to be safe to enter there and Helen could see now that the hatches had become encrusted and joined to the main shelf of coral. It was true that the strands were tenuous enough to be easily broken, but the frigate was right on the edge of the shelf even now and it wouldn't take a great deal to send her over the edge and down into water where it would be too deep to follow her.

Helen moved from her first position to where Gregory had tried to cut away the side of the frigate. It was obviously a long, slow job and it was obvious too that he needed help. She wondered if they had already decided to make their entrance that way when Michael had been there, but she doubted it. All the work looked too recent for that.

She had been down a good time now. The fish accepted her presence and swam in and out of her arms and legs casually as they did through the branches of coral that surrounded them. She was playing with a small green fish that blew itself up until she thought it would burst when she stroked its back, when she noticed that Gregory had come down to join her. He tapped his watch significantly and pointed towards the surface. Helen glanced down at her own watch and was astonished to see that she had only ten minutes of compressed air left. She breathed deeply to facilitate her rise to the surface, enjoying the bubbles that spun out from her breathing apparatus and danced up to the surface ahead of her. Then at last she broke through the surface and could feel the heat of the sun on her face. A second later Gregory was there beside her, and they had both whipped off their masks and had wrenched the air nozzles out of their mouths. To Helen's inexpressible relief, Gregory was smiling.

"Well?" she challenged him.

He shook his head so violently that drops of water sprayed all over her. "It was a nice, cosy dive," he agreed. "Now we must get down to some work. Come on board and I'll explain what I'm aiming at."

Helen needed no second invitation. She climbed aboard, as agile as she had always been, and stood watching the water drip off her on to the deck, laughing with a sudden warm gaiety that she hadn't heard from herself for a long, long time.

"I take it you enjoyed yourself?" Gregory suggested, amused.

"I certainly did! I'd almost forgotten what a feeling of freedom diving gives one."

"It's hard work too," he warned her.

She shook out her hair and grinned. "Who's afraid of hard work?" she retorted.

"Now that's what I like to hear, a dedicated woman," he drawled. Helen wasn't sure how to take that, so she didn't bother to answer. She followed him meekly down into the cabin and looked at the plans he spread out on the table for her benefit, trying not to drip water all over them. It was clear that formerly the frigate had lain the right way up and she wondered what had happened to turn her on to her side, as she was lying now.

"When did you start to cut your way in through the metal plates?" she asked.

"After Michael—" Gregory broke off, his face

solemn and angry. "No matter, it's what we have to deal with now that matters. And we don't want anyone rocking the boat from now on, or she'll fall off the ledge altogether. You can see that, can't you?"

Helen nodded. "You have all the equipment?" she checked with him.

"Enough. I've been trying to do it all myself so far. It's been a difficult season and the weather was against me too. It's difficult to believe now what it can be like in the rainy season and what can happen when a typhoon comes along!"

"Here?" Helen exclaimed, surprised. "I didn't know there were any extremes here in the Islands!" She blushed, conscious that she was exposing her ignorance to eyes that might well not be kindly. "I'd imagined that the weather was always like it is today," she finished lamely.

"I suppose it mostly is," he agreed equably enough. "But when it does choose to do something different, it's pretty wholehearted about it. The rains go on and on for weeks when they come. The typhoons are usually short, sharp and unpleasant, but we get warning of them now, so it isn't as bad as it was once."

He turned away from the maps abruptly and got out the blowlamp equipment, which was so designed and fuelled that it worked well under water.

"Have you used this before?" he asked her.

Helen shook her head. "But I'll learn," she said eagerly.

"We'll see," he answered dryly. He went on to explain exactly how it was to be used and she repeated the lesson like a half-witted child until she felt she would burst if he made her go through it even once again.

"You may be impatient now," he told her, "but things look different down there. You can burn yourself pretty badly and do untold damage to your breathing

48

equipment. If you don't know exactly what to do, it can be the difference between life and death."

He was right, of course. She admitted that. But she could well imagine how Michael would have reacted to being told the obvious again and again by a man who didn't even trouble to wear shoes around the Islands. And yet she couldn't fault him when it came to his administration of the salvage operation. That worried her too, she admitted to herself, for she could well imagine. Michael underrating such a man. She might have done so herself if she hadn't been startled into awareness by the animal attraction the man had for her. She was so aware of him that she couldn't possibly miss the dedication he had for his job under that lazy, charming buccaneer exterior, but as for Michael she couldn't be sure. She racked her brains trying to remember what he had written to her about Gregory de Vaux, but she could remember nothing that wasn't the merest platitude. Oh, Michael, she thought, was that why you died?

"Are you ready to go down again?" Gregory broke into her thoughts, his voice edgy with his distaste for using a woman for such a task.

"Yes, I'm quite ready," she said.

She took more care this time with her preparations and she was glad that she had when the sea closed over her head and she was alone in the silent world where man was a stranger and would be until the end of his days.

The equipment was more difficult to use than she had expected. She was thankful that Gregory had made it easier by numbering the various things she had to do to get the flame hot enough to eat into the encrusted metal she was attempting to cut. It was a long, hard process. If they could have taken the frigate up to the surface, she supposed it would have taken them only a few hours, but here, under the water, every inch was an advance and a personal triumph. The currents in the water that she had been scarcely aware of before pulled at the lamp and her arms shook with the effort of holding the flame steady enough for it to heat and eat away a passage through the metal.

As it was she looked at her watch more often than she had ever done in a mere half hour under water, thinking that her time down there would never be done. When she came slowly up to the surface, she was more tired than she would have cared to admit. It was sheer grit and determination that had seen her through, and she only hoped that Gregory didn't know it as clearly as she did herself.

He helped her on board in silence and she hoped she didn't look as green as she felt. "Well?" he said at last.

Helen slid her cylinders of compressed air on to the deck, suddenly conscious of their unbearable weight once she was out of the water. "It was hard work," she agreed frankly. "But not too hard. I'll manage it and I'll see that you don't regret employing me. Is that fair enough?"

He looked at her closely and for a long moment she thought .that he was going to refuse her. "It's day in, day out until we get that gold up," he reminded her.

She jutted out her chin in a way that would have been familiar to her whole family. Once Helen had made up her mind, she would die sooner than not carry out what she had decided on. "So?" she asked coolly.

"So I shall expect as much from you as from myself," he said sternly.

"It's a deal," she answered with a lightness she was far from feeling.

He held out a hand to her and she shook it. She felt cold and a little sick from reaction, but she was proud enough not to allow him to see how much his approbation meant to her.

"There's my sister-in-law as well," she said gruffly.

His eyebrows shot up. "What has that got to do with me?" he demanded.

Helen picked up her bathrobe and wrapped it about her, rubbing herself dry as she did so. "When she comes, she'll have to do something," she said. "It's—it's a package deal."

Gregory sat down on the roof of the saloon behind him and stared at her. "Isn't it enough that I'm employing you?" he raged at her. "A woman to do a man's job! And I wouldn't do that, let me tell you, if I could get anyone else! And now you tell me I have to employ some other female as well. And not just another woman, but another *Hastings*!"

Helen wound her hair round her finger, wishing that her heart wouldn't beat so loudly that he must hear it and know exactly how nervous she was.

"You'll like Anita," she said in a funny, flat voice.

"Okay," he said. "What can she do?"

Helen looked perplexed, then swallowed hard. "I—I don't know," she admitted. "Perhaps she could buy in the provisions?"

"Ye gods!"

"You don't understand," Helen went on desperately. "She's never done anything—ever! All she's ever done is follow Mrs. Hastings about like a shadow. That's why we came," she ended lamely.

Gregory de Vaux opened his mouth to say something and shut it again. He made a defeated gesture with his hands, smiling finally at his own defeat. "Okay she buys the provisions," he said. "She can get anything she wants through the hotel. But she does *not* bother me on board! Is that a deal?"

Helen nodded, too relieved even to say a word.

"Nor can I afford to pay her more than pocket money," Gregory went on grimly. "You will receive exactly what I paid Michael." His eyes met hers relentlessly. "What you do with it is your own affair, but if you do a man's job you'll receive a man's pay. Now for heaven's sake, get inside and get some clothing on. You make me feel that I'm conducting a kindergarten

rather than a diving contract with you in that robe—
and I don't like the feeling!" he added violently.

She went so quickly that she nearly tripped over her
own feet going down the narrow companionway. She
didn't like working with him much, come to that,
either, but at least she had too much sense to say so.
She sniffed, admiring her own restraint. A kindergarten
indeed! Why, yes she'd show him. Oh yes, Mr.
Gregory de Vaux, she'd show him! Then she laughed
and, for some awful reason she couldn't explain to
herself, she couldn't stop, and then she was crying with
the tears pouring down her face. And she *never* cried,
she never had, not even when she had first heard that
Michael was dead.

By the time she had finished dressing, she was exhausted and completely sober. But at least she had a
job. She sat in the saloon and sipped Taine-Mal's
coffee, telling herself over again that she had the job.
She was quite surprised when Gregory came down the
companionway and told her they had tied up at the
jetty in the harbour.

"Come on," he said gently. "Miss Corrigan will be
waiting for you, to feed you and put you to bed!"

"I can manage by myself!" she rapped back at him.

"I guess you can at that!" he admitted easily. "But
tomorrow is another day, you know. Goodnight, Helen
Hastings, sleep well!"

She jumped ashore on to the uneven jetty and
turned to look back at him, but he was already busy
tidying up the diving tackle on the deck. Well, what
more did she expect for a man's wage, she asked herself
angrily; to be walked home to her own front door? She
took a deep breath and, holding her head up high, she
walked back to the hotel—alone.

# CHAPTER FOUR

MISS CORRIGAN was busily engaged in tearing up portions of bread and dropping them into her soup. When she had finished, she huffed and puffed with elaborate satisfaction, then picked up her spoon to take the first, luxurious sip.

"You should have had some too!" she said to Helen.

Helen shook her head wearily. "I couldn't!" she exclaimed.

"Don't know a good thing when you see it!" the old lady complained. "*That's* the trouble with young people today! It has nothing to do with violence and all these things, it's nothing more than a proper discrimination for the good things of life!"

Helen smiled. "But I really wouldn't enjoy it!" she protested.

Miss Corrigan's eyes looked at her shrewdly across the table. "What are you going to eat?" she asked her. "You have to eat something! I'll order some wine for you to be getting on with." She was as good as her word, pouring out the golden liquid she had chosen with a flourish into first Helen's glass and then her own. "Well, my dear, to your new job! May you find what you came for!"

Helen could feel the wine warming her and making her relax. "I came because of Anita," she said mildly.

"And that husband of yours had nothing to do with it?"

"Not much," Helen said firmly. She kept telling herself that that was true, but she supposed that it couldn't be, not entirely, for why else had she come right across the world if not to find out exactly how he had died? Only it wasn't for the reasons they all thought. She wanted to be free of him, free of his memory, and free of the last ties that bound her to him.

"You don't think Anita will be bored here when she does come?" the old lady went on. "There isn't much here for her to do, is there?"

"Oh, I don't know," Helen answered easily. "She's never been out of England before and it will take her some time to explore the Islands, I should think. Besides," she added blandly, "Gregory is going to give her a job, buying in all the provisions and things like that."

Miss Corrigan stopped drinking her soup. Her mouth sagged with surprise and she stared at Helen as though the girl were some figment of her imagination. "Are you sure?" she asked with awe.

"It's part of our agreement," Helen confirmed.

"He must be going soft in the head!" Miss Corrigan exclaimed.

Helen grinned. "I think he needs help rather badly," she said. "He wouldn't say so, but I knew the minute I went down and looked at the frigate."

"Well, I knew that!" Miss Corrigan said doubtfully. "He certainly wouldn't have thought of taking you on otherwise. He's lucky to get you, I know, but he doesn't know that yet. But *Anita,* that's a different kettle of fish!"

"Well, actually, I didn't give him much choice," Helen admitted. "I said it was both of us or nothing. I thought for a while it was going to be nothing, but in the end he agreed to taking us both on."

The waiter came and took Miss Corrigan's soup plate away, bringing a large dish of lobster along for them both, which he set in the centre of the table, grinning with pleasure at the look on their faces.

"Mr. Harmon say, telephone for you, missy," he

told Helen. "Telephone on and off all day. No answer except you personally. Shall I say you here now?"

Helen glanced across the table to Miss Corrigan for guidance. She didn't understand if she was wanted that minute, or whether they had made arrangements to ring back, or what.

"Finish your food first, dear," Miss Corrigan recommended. "You can take the call later. If they've been phoning all day, they'll wait."

Helen did as she was advised, but she was anxious all through dinner, wondering who could possibly be telephoning her when hardly anyone knew she was there.

"It's Anita!" she said at last. "It must be! Could she telephone from New Zealand? Something must have gone wrong! Oh dear, do you suppose there've been some complications with her appendicitis?"

"Most unlikely!" Miss Corrigan grunted. "I'd say it was far more likely that she's been given a date when she can come out of hospital. Relax, child, you'll give yourself indigestion if you go on like that. Probably give it to me too," she added grimly. "At my age, one's comfort is permanently at risk if one eats the things one enjoys!"

Helen gulped down the rest of her meal and hurried to the manager's office where the waiter said she could receive the call. Peter Harmon was waiting for her, smiling a gentle welcome.

"I hear you got the job with Gregory de Vaux all right," he congratulated her. "Did you manage to get along with him at all? Most people find him quite a tyrant on that boat of his!"

"He's efficient," Helen said guardedly.

"He's efficient when he's off the boat!" Peter grimaced, and Helen wondered what the occasion had been when he had run foul of Gregory. She couldn't imagine it, for Peter's manner was so very inoffensive that she couldn't imagine him upsetting anyone.

"Did the call come from New Zealand?" she asked him anxiously as he sat on the edge of his desk and dialled a number.

"Yeah. Weren't you expecting it?"

"It must be my sister-in-law," Helen said. "I do hope there's nothing wrong!"

Peter Harmon grinned at her over the receiver. "Oh, I don't think anything's wrong!" he said cheerfully. "I took the call earlier. It was someone who sounded young and pretty. Would that be your sister-in-law? I told her she'd be mighty welcome when she did make it our way!"

He had a long running conversation with the exchange which went on and on, while Helen waited as patiently as she could for him to finish.

"She's on the line now!" he said at last. She took the receiver from him and practically shouted "Hullo" down the mouthpiece.

"Helen?" Anita's voice answered her gaily. "Helen, I'm flying to Melonga tomorrow. I've been out of the hospital for a couple of days and it seems the plane is going tomorrow. It will be the same pilot who took you!"

"But, Anita!" Helen said weakly. "Do you feel well enough?"

"Of course I do! What do you imagine having your appendix out is like? Well, I can tell you, it's a piece of cake!"

Helen had never heard the other girl sound so vital or so *gay*. She pictured the Anita she knew with rather straggly mouse-coloured hair and nothing very much to say for herself, and wondered what could have happened to make her feel so lively now.

"Can you meet me?" Anita went on, bubbling over with excitement.

"I don't know!" Helen said uncertainly. "Look,

56

Anita, the airstrip is on a different island from the hotel. Will you wait there until I can arrange for a boat to pick you up?"

"Anything," Anita said happily. "I'm bringing lots of film for my camera, so I shall be quite happy anywhere at all."

Helen blinked. She hadn't known about the camera either. "Good," she said. "As a matter of fact, I have some news too. I got the job—you know, the one Michael had. I've got a job for you too!"

"For me?" The note in Anita's voice changed dramatically. "Oh, Helen, is it something I can do? I mean, I wouldn't want to let you down. It isn't at all difficult, is it?

"No," said Helen briefly. "It's only buying a few stores. You can do that, can't you?"

"I—I don't know. Who for?"

"For Gregory de Vaux. He has a Polynesian who does most of the cooking and so on, but someone is needed to get stores from the hotel and so on."

"Oh well," Anita said, a little more cheerful now that the job had been defined, "perhaps I could manage that. If Mr. de Vaux isn't too demanding. D-do you like him, Helen?"

Helen wondered if she liked him or not and found herself quite unable to say. "He's all right," she said awkwardly.

Anita uttered a little hushed gasp. "I shouldn't have asked you!" she exclaimed remorsefully. "I'd forgotten for the moment—"

"Forgotten what?" Helen asked impatiently.

"Michael and all that," Anita rushed on. "I mean, it must make a difference, mustn't it?"

"Why?" Helen put in quickly.

"Well, I don't suppose other men seem the same," Anita said innocently. "I wish I hadn't said anything at all!"

"So do I," Helen agreed angrily. She thought she

could hear Anita trying ineffectually to muzzle a sob and wished she could think of something comforting to say. She knew that Anita was expecting her to say that it was true, that she was missing Michael and that it would be years before she got over his absence from her life, but she didn't feel anything of the sort.

"Are you cross, Helen?" Anita's voice asked anxiously.

"No, dear, not a bit," Helen answered. "I'm looking forward to seeing you. But are you sure you're fit enough to travel? It isn't very comfortable on that freight plane."

"I'm fine!" Anita insisted. "I'll be seeing you. Goodbye for now."

"Goodbye," Helen responded. "Until tomorrow." She replaced the receiver in its rest and stared moodily down at it until she became aware of Peter's cough in the doorway to warn her of his presence.

"Finished?" he asked her.

She nodded. "It was my sister-in-law. You were quite right."

Peter Harmon looked pleased. "And she's coming here?"

Helen nodded again. "Look," she said, "I've persuaded Gregory to give Anita a job getting all our provisions and things. Gregory said she could do that through the hotel. Will that be all right?"

"Sure. Why not?" He sounded cool and a bit distant.

"Will it be a trouble for you?" Helen pressed him, wondering why he didn't sound a little more enthusiastic.

"No, no trouble." He hesitated. "I was only wondering if your sister-in-law didn't want to find her own job? I'd maybe have given her one. Does she want to have it all laid out for her?"

Helen was frankly astonished. "You don't understand," she said. "You've never met Anita. She's never been away from her mother before and—"

"And now you know best what's good for her?" Peter suggested. He said it so charmingly that Helen couldn't possibly have taken offence.

"I hadn't thought about it like that," she admitted. "But I think I do. At first, anyway. You'll see tomorrow when she comes. You'll help her, won't you? You see, she hasn't any confidence in herself and more than anything else I want this whole trip to be a success for her."

Peter Harmon smiled at her formally. "The hotel will do all it can to help, you can be sure of that, Mrs. Hastings. I'll see to it personally."

Helen felt oddly defeated as she thanked him and left his office to go back into the main part of the hotel, to where Miss Corrigan had ordered coffee for them both on the terrace. Outsiders, she thought, people who didn't know the Hastings well, would never understand how nervous Anita was, how her confidence had been sapped away by her mother. She sighed. She supposed that it did look as though she were being a busybody and over-protective, but what else could she do? Anita had to be given her chance, and she was going to give it to her, no matter what anyone else thought or did!

Helen had to run to the jetty the following morning, for she was afraid she would be late. When she had woken in her splendid bedroom to find the sun already lighting up the peacock colours on the chair opposite her and knew that it was late. From then on it had been a mad rush to get herself ready for the long day out on the *Sweet Promise*.

"The Boss is waiting for you!" Na-Tinn called out to her. "Here, jump aboard here!"

Obediently, Helen cast herself into the air and landed beside him in a heap on the narrow deck. His strong arms rescued her from falling backwards into the sea, his grinning teeth a great deal nearer to her than she quite liked.

"Very good morning!" he laughed happily.

"Very!" she agreed, rather less sure than he had been.

"Ah, there you are!" Gregory greeted her from the top of the companionway. "I thought you were going to be late," he said dryly.

"So did I," Helen admitted ruefully. "I overslept."

His face softened into a smile. "It happens to all of us. I expect you were tired—"

Helen's head went up sharply. "Not too tired!" she interrupted him quickly, just in case he should think that the diving was going to be beyond her. "My sister-in-law rang up from New Zealand. She's— she's coming today—"

"And you want us to pick her up on the way back?" he finished for her.

She nodded hopefully. "If it isn't too much trouble," she said anxiously.

"It won't have to be!" he grunted. "We can hardly leave her on an uninhabited island all night! Have you told her she'll have a bit of a wait?"

"Yes. She doesn't mind at all."

"Well, that's something! Come on then, if we have to be back early, we'd better get going. Check the equipment, will you, while I cast off and make sure we're going in the right direction."

Helen squashed past him to get down the companionway, thinking that she was not the only one who had woken up that morning with an edge to her temper. She was sorry that it had to be her first full day at work that Anita had come. It would have been easier to ask him to collect her at any time other than right at the beginning. It almost looked as if she had been waiting to get the job before bringing her sister-in-law to the Melonga Islands at all. She tried to persuade herself that it didn't matter what he thought, but at the back of her mind she knew that it did. They would be on top of one another from dawn to dusk for many days to come and it would be easier if they could like and respect one another and, judging from this morning's experience, it hardly looked as though he were going to suffer her gladly at all!

It was hot by the time they reached the wreck of the frigate. Helen wedged herself between the cabins and the deck-rail and began to climb into her diving gear. The flippers were a size too large for her, but she managed to tighten them behind her heels so that there was no danger of them falling off. Taine-Mal helped her to strap the cylinders of compressed air on to her back and she fixed the belt that held the lead weights around her waist. As always she felt weighed down by the sheer weight of what she had to carry and couldn't wait to get into the water when the load would magically turn into nothing and the lovely clear water would flow free about her.

On the other side of the *Sweet Promise*, Gregory was getting ready too. He had the cutting equipment with him and was carefully winding the tubes that carried the oxygen down to the blowlamp round a wooden barrel to keep them from getting twisted and tied into knots.

"Are you ready?" he asked her when he had finished and the *Sweet Promise* was safely anchored above the wreck. She caught a glimpse of the real concern in his eyes and realised suddenly just how anxious he was about her diving with him.

"I'm ready," she said. She felt grotesque and awkward as she struggled down the side of the boat and into the water, but once there, she waited for him to join her, swimming out strongly to get out of his way as he entered the water beside her.

The metal-cutting equipment was handed down to them and the Polynesian sailors began unwinding the oxygen pipes that would keep them going deep down under the water. Gregory smiled briefly at Helen, placed his mask more securely over his eyes and nose and disappeared beneath the water. In a few seconds Helen had followed him, allowing herself to sink down and down until she was level with the frigate before she pulled herself along the coral shelf to where it was lying.

Gregory took one of the lamps and started cutting through the metal plate she had been working on the day before. Helen came to a standing position on top of the fractured metal of the wrecked ship and prepared herself to attack the place from the other end. Gregory handed her a lighted lamp and she started work. It was queer to see the flame burning through the water to reach the metal. It gave it a peculiar blue light, but it was pretty effective all the same. In half an hour they had cut their way through one side of the square that Gregory had marked on the hull, and he signalled to her that that was enough for one session and that it was time for them to surface. She nodded her agreement and turned out the flame she had been using, wedging the blowlamp into a coral ridge that was conveniently handy and which held it securely.

Gregory struck out for the surface and she watched his long, lean sunburned body. She knew that she ought to follow him, but she was tempted to swim right round the wreck, to move her stiff muscles and get the blood flowing again after the long time she had spent standing still in the water.

When she looked more closely at the frigate than she had the day before, she could see how badly fractured it had been when it had run aground on the reef. The whole of the front was twisted and dangerous. Worse, she suspected that underneath, somewhere in the side that was now lying on the shelf, there was a gaping hole which had caused the frigate to founder and sink. Anxious to find out, she swam as close as she could to the twisted metal, avoiding the jagged pieces that threatened any approach. She was small enough to pull herself right into one of the gaps between the ship and the coral bed and then she was sure that she was right. There was a large black hole in the metal, not big enough for her to get through now, though it must have been amply big enough before the ship had turned on to its side.

Helen shone her torch into the black interior and caught a glimpse of space and further darkness. How odd it was, she thought, that the hole was so neat. It was the only place where the metal edges were not jagged or sharp. Here, they were smooth and worn, almost as if they had been carefully designed and cut neatly out of the hull. Could someone have been there before them? she wondered. But that was scarcely possible. The Islanders would have noticed and reported anybody who had been seen messing about with the wreck. They all knew that the gold it contained belonged to them, the wages for a whole year's work in the copra plantations. Yet she was as certain as she could be that someone had deliberately made that hole, that it was not a freak holing that had resulted in the carefully even sides.

She was on her way back to the surface when she first thought that perhaps the hole had been made before the frigate had run on to the reef. She was not an expert in such matters, but she could imagine that the frigate, thus holed, could have run a fair way before actually foundering. Perhaps the hole could even have been made while the frigate had been in harbour, before it had even set sail. Was it possible? She shrugged the whole idea away from her as she reached the surface and broke through the gay patterns the sun was making on the surface of the water. In a normal world of sun and sea, the fantasies of the deep seemed even more impossible. Who would want to hole the frigate? There wasn't anyone who could possibly have benefited from such an action! She was daft even to have allowed such an idea to cross her mind.

Gregory himself helped her on board the *Sweet Promise*. He had already cast off his own equipment and was wearing a towelling jacket of emerald green that suited him better than anything she had seen him in. With his damp hair curling in the sun, he looked very handsome and even more dangerous to her peace of mind.

"It took you a long time to come up," he said.

"I was just looking around," she answered him. His eyes narrowed a trifle.

"Indeed? Why?"

She shrugged her shoulders, laughing. "Just to see what's there!" she told him. "Why else?"

"It's dangerous down there," he said flatly. "And I don't want that frigate turning any further."

She shivered. "I should think not! Was it ever the right way up? Or did it lie like that from the beginning? It seems so odd to me that it should have practically turned turtle."

"We had a bit of difficulty down there," Gregory answered her guardedly. "She shifted quite a bit and the entrance we had made was useless. So be careful! Any movement down there might knock her off that shelf!"

Helen longed to ask him if Michael had been there when she had shifted that last time, but she didn't like to bring up the subject of her dead husband again. They seemed to get on a great deal better when Michael was forgotten, she thought wryly, and pulled her bathrobe on over her shoulders, staring down over the side of the boat into the deep green waters that surrounded them.

She looked over her shoulder and grinned at him. "I am careful!" she said.

"Is that so?" he drawled. "You don't seem the careful type to me!"

"Well," she said, "since we're being personal, you don't to me either!"

His look of astonishment amused her. "Indeed? Well, don't let it throw you," he retorted. "I'm careful all right, especially when it comes to my work. I don't approve of people fooling around with that sort of thing."

She wondered if that was meant as a warning to her. "My father didn't fool about either," she answered sharply. "I don't think I've given you any cause for complaint so far, have I?"

"Not so far," he grinned at her. "D'you want something to eat?"

She accepted the sandwich he held out to her and a mug of hot coffee, and sat down contentedly on the roof of the cabin, allowing the sun and the food to warm her through.

"Of course," she went on innocently, "if I had ever seen you in a pair of shoes, I might have a quite different impression—"

He laughed. "So you believe that clothes make the man, do you?"

"No-o," she said softly, "but they help somewhat, don't you think?"

Gregory stretched himself along the top of the cabin beside her, smiling to himself. "I'll not be drawn on that topic," he said firmly. "Tell me about this sister of yours. Is she anything like you?"

"Not a bit!" she assured him. "She's a gentle little creature—"

"Ah now, that I'm glad to hear!" he put in at once. "I prefer my women that way. Is she pretty?"

Helen wondered why she should feel so disappointed. It was quite unreasonable of her to take his teasing seriously, she told herself. "Yes, she's pretty," she said in an off-hand voice. "In a pale sort of way."

"Oh well," he said, "I'll be able to judge for myself soon enough. It's practically time for the next session. We'd better start to get ready."

They worked hard all afternoon. Helen thought that

Gregory had reason to be pleased with their progress. Between them they had practically cut through the first layer of the hull of the frigate. With another day's work they should be able to pull the plate away and start on the inside skin. In a week, they ought to be inside the ship and looking for the gold. If he was pleased, he gave no sign, however. He seemed almost reluctant to give the order to return to harbour, annoyed by the time they wasted each day going back and forth.

"If you were a man I'd have you sleeping on board as Michael did," he told her. "We'd save a couple of hours each day."

"I wouldn't mind," she said. "There are enough bunks for Anita to have one too, if necessary."

He looked at her in sudden appreciation. "That might be an idea!" he responded enthusiastically. "I'll think about it."

He went aft to start the engine up and shouted to the Polynesians to lift the anchor and to get ready to take them back again. Na-Tinn ran round the boat like a scalded cat, his unfailing grin very much in evidence as he pulled up the sails to catch the evening breeze, singing softly under his breath some ancient song that his ancestors must have sung several hundreds of years before. It had a bright catchy tune, and after a few minutes Taine-Mal joined in, his big voice carrying for miles across the still water. Helen found herself humming the tune too, adding a sweeter, feminine note to the deep bass of the others.

"Very good!" Taine-Mal said appreciatively. "Very nice song too."

"What's it about?" Helen asked him.

He creased up his forehead in his efforts to translate the words for her. "It's about a man who goes on a long journey. It will be years before he returns. He leaves his beloved behind, but one day he will come back to her."

Helen thought of how the Polynesian people had

crossed the Pacific Ocean in their tiny boats, steering back and forth by the stars, and she marvelled at their courage.

"We come to the airstrip now," he told her as a companionable silence fell between them. "We go in, no?"

Helen stood up, holding on with one hand round the mast to keep her balance. She thought she could make out the tiny figure of Anita standing where she had stood only two days before. The figure grew larger as they drew nearer and she was jumping up and down in her excitement.

"Here, have mercy on that canvas!" Gregory rebuked her.

Helen chuckled. Nothing could damp her good humour at that moment. She waved eagerly to Anita, but there was no answering wave. Indeed, when they got close enough to make out each other's features, she thought for a moment that she had made a mistake and that it wasn't Anita at all, but then she saw that it was, but it was an Anita she had never seen before. This was an Anita with carefully permed hair and a tailored coat that fitted her well enough to have been bought for her rather than inherited from her mother. This was an Anita who looked suddenly well-groomed and not a bit pale and stringy.

"Anita!" she exclaimed.

Anita smiled and blushed, plainly self-conscious in her new finery. And then she saw Gregory and Gregory saw her, and her smile grew wider. "You must be Mr. de Vaux," she said in a pretty, soft voice that Helen was sure she had never heard before. "I heard so much about you from my brother. He was *such* an admirer of yours!"

Helen cast Gregory an astonished glance, but apparently he found nothing grotesque about such a statement at all! He was looking at Anita as though his eyes were about to pop out of his head.

"My word," he said, "I wish your brother had returned the compliment, Miss Hastings. It would take a long time to grow tired of hearing about you!"

"Why, thank you," Anita smiled gently. "Do you think you could possibly help me to come on board?"

# CHAPTER FIVE

"NOT in those shoes!" Helen exclaimed. "Take them off, Anita! These decks are made of canvas. You'd go straight through them!"

Anita gulped guiltily. "I suppose I ought to have chunky heels," she said shyly. "They're all the rage now, aren't they? But somehow the fine heel seems so much more flattering to one's feet. What do you think, Mr. de Vaux?"

Gregory grinned. "I think they do great things for your feet!" he agreed readily. "But Helen's right. Not to worry, I expect your bare feet are a pretty sight too!"

Helen stared hard at them both. She wouldn't have believed it! Not if half the population of the Islands had told her, she wouldn't have believed it. That Anita could have turned out a *flirt* was too much! And to think that she, Helen, had brought her here to instil a little confidence into her.

Anita obediently took off her shoes and stood on the deck with her hands clasped behind her back, looking more than a little helpless. "I've never been on a boat like this before. I think it's *sweet*!"

Gregory looked gratified. "She's a pretty good little tub," he said. "Why don't you go below with Helen and I'll give you both a drink?"

Anita hugged herself with glee. "I'd love that!" she giggled.

Helen went first down the narrow companionway into the saloon. She knew she had nothing to be furious about, but she felt furious all the same. She felt *cheated*. Anita wasn't even now a raving beauty, but she certainly wasn't the pale, stringy girl that

Helen had known her sister-in-law to be. Of course, anyone who had been forced to live any length of time with that mother of hers would have become paler and stringier by the minute, even so the change that had come over Anita was quite phenomenal. If she were more generous, Helen told herself sternly, she would congratulate Anita on the change. As it was, she couldn't understand her own resentment at the transformation, except that she knew that it had something to do with the look on Gregory's face, and that in itself was ridiculous! Why should she care how he looked at anyone? Anyone at all?

Ashamed of herself, Helen set herself to making Anita feel at home. She hid her surprise when Gregory produced a bottle of Australian wine, managing to look as if she had expected something like this all along. She held the plastic tumblers that were the only receptacles that they could find while Gregory poured the rose-coloured sparkling liquid into them, and her hands didn't shake one bit. She passed Anita one of the tumblers and smiled at her.

"Well," she said, "how was New Zealand?"

Anita's eyes sparkled with enthusiasm. "It was lovely!" she sighed. "I know it was being in hospital and all that, but it was so peaceful! I never thought life could be like that before!"

There was no doubt about it, Helen decided to herself, she was a cad. How could she resent whatever pleasure Anita could get out of life on this side of the world?

"So it wasn't too bad, having your appendix out?" she murmured.

Anita leaned forward, smiling gently. "I *enjoyed* it, Helen. I really enjoyed it. The operation was nothing! It didn't even hurt! And the nurses were so good to me! It was they who took me out shopping and made me get my hair done too. Do you like it?"

Helen's eyes softened. "I love it!" she said warmly. "I hardly recognised you at first!"

Anita blushed prettily. She turned to Gregory with a quick, apologetic gesture. "You should have seen me before!" she told him. "You mustn't mind Helen teasing me a bit. My mother didn't approve of any aids to beauty," she added earnestly.

"For other people," Helen added dryly.

Anita's eyes widened dramatically. "Do you mean to say—" she began. "I suppose she *must* have," she went on thoughtfully. "But you must admit that she did it most frightfully well!"

"Oh yes, I'll grant you that!" Helen agreed lazily.

Gregory grinned at them both. "There doesn't seem to be much love lost between you and the old lady," he said suddenly. "I always got the impression that Michael was quite fond of her."

Anita looked quite abashed. "Oh, we shouldn't have said anything!" she said, acutely embarrassed. "I'd forgotten for the moment that you don't know her. You have made me feel so very much at home, you see. I'm so sorry!"

"You don't have to apologise to me," he said easily. "I was surprised, that's all."

Helen sat up very straight, making herself as tall as possible. "You wouldn't be if you ever met her," she said solemnly. "She is—she's *awful!*"

He laughed. "A typical mother-in-law?" he suggested.

Helen frowned. "Hardly that!" she muttered.

Gregory looked surprised. "I believe you really mean it! Didn't you like her at all?"

Helen shivered despite herself. "No, I can't say I did," she said.

"It's all right for you," Anita put in with a sad smile. "You don't have to go back to her. I have to keep remembering that I'm only here for a time.

When it's all over, I shall go back to England, and that will be that! I'll never have any life of my own ever again!" Her eyes filled with tears and she sniffed pathetically. "Never mind, I shall make the best of the time I have," she added bravely. "And —I'll work very hard for you, Mr. de Vaux."

"I'm sure you will," he agreed in kind tones. He stood up, ducking his head so that he didn't hit it on the upper deck. "I'd better go above and see what's happening. Helen will tell you about the Islands and what you need to know, I expect. I'll be seeing you." He went off, whistling a catchy little tune under his breath.

Damn the man, thought Helen. It was unnecessary for him to be so attractive! Now he had Anita catching her breath whenever he hove over the horizon as well as—no, she was not going to admit that he affected her in any way at all! She would not!

"Oh, Helen, it's so lovely to see you!" Anita exclaimed as soon as Gregory had gone. "You look a wee bit tired, if you don't mind my saying so. Do you have to work most frightfully hard?"

Helen pokered up. She hadn't noticed how tired she was and she didn't *want* to notice. With Anita looking so pretty and gay, the last thing she wanted was a picture of herself as worn out, with her hair sticky from salt water, and with precious little control over her emotions to boot! How odd it was, she thought dispassionately, that having spent all this time since Michael's death in an emotional limbo, she was now as edgy as a young girl waiting for her first date. She would have to do better than that, she told herself sternly, if she was going to be any good to Anita—or be able to do the job she had undertaken. She sighed. She had forgotten what painful things emotions could be. She had been much better off without them.

"Helen, you're not listening! What are you dreaming about? My, I thought I was the dreamy one! Don't you think Mr. de Vaux is a dreamboat of a man? Is he always as kind as he has been today? I thought you found him rather unyielding—you know, that he didn't like women much—"

"Whatever made you think that?" Helen put in quickly.

Anita considered the point. "I don't know," she said at last. "It was something you said on the phone. Then you do like him?"

Helen shrugged her shoulders. "He's all right," she said inadequately.

"*All right!*" Anita screamed with laughter. "Helen have you *looked* at him? I think he's beautiful! *Really* beautiful!"

"You're just starry-eyed about everything," Helen told her firmly. "You wait until he's yelling at you because you've forgotten something that he needs at that particular moment!"

Anita looked prim. "I don't believe he would yell at anyone!" she defended him, quite cross that Helen should make such a suggestion.

"Oh, wouldn't he!" Helen retorted.

"Even if he does," Anita continued defensively, "it would only be because you deserved it. I'm sure of that! I think he's as nice as anything!"

Helen sighed. "Good," she said finally. She cleared away their glasses, pumping up some water into the sink to wash them up. The *Sweet Promise* was the most beautifully equipped boat she had ever been on, she reflected. With a little money spent on her, to provide a few luxurious touches and to paint her outside and in, and she would be worthy of a millionaire and smart trips around the Mediterranean. Perhaps it was as well that she had to earn her living after all, for here, in the Pacific, she had to do that or Gregory wouldn't have been able to keep her.

"Helen," Anita said suddenly, her voice breathless and dismayed. "Oh, Helen, do you think I could possibly be seasick?"

Helen turned and looked at her with alarm. It was true that she looked more than a little green. "You'd better go on deck," she advised briskly. "Do you think you can get that far?"

Anita nodded desperately. She ran to the companionway and hurried up the narrow steps with Helen close behind her.

Taine-Mal looked first of all anxious and then, when he saw what was happening, he roared with laughter with the full-throated laugh of the Polynesian. Anita gave him a look of dislike mixed with fear. "D-did you see his teeth?" she shuddered, holding Helen's arm so tightly that it hurt.

"Hush, he'll hear you," Helen whispered.

"I don't care if he does!"

"But I care," Gregory said relentlessly. He had come towards them, his feet completely silent on the canvas deck. "What's the matter? Helen, get her below! Haven't we got enough amateurs playing at working on board this boat, without having bad sailors amongst them? Well, haven't we?"

Helen bravely stood her ground. "If you're referring to me," she said distinctly, "I reckon I gave you a pretty fair day's work today."

Gregory relaxed, the tautness leaving him as suddenly as it had come. "You're right, of course," he apologised. "You mustn't mind me. I find employing females an added responsibility I hadn't looked for, that's all."

Helen turned her back on him, to show her disapproval more clearly. "We can look after ourselves!" she said.

"Are you sure?" She knew he was laughing at

her, but she didn't care. She was there and so was Anita, and that, for the moment, was enough for her.

"We're quite sure!" she said.

His laughter followed her down the companionway making her feel uncomfortable. In fact, she had quite forgotten what had taken them on deck in the first place until she caught a glimpse of Anita's pale face. "Are you feeling any better?" she asked her, wondering at her own lack of sympathy that her attention should have been distracted so easily.

"A little," Anita said uncertainly. She took a deep breath. "Who is that man?" she added in a hushed voice.

Helen smiled. "He's one of the Polynesian sailors. They're two brothers. You mustn't mind them, they're very good at their work. And they're so jolly!" she added, remembering their easy laughter.

"But his teeth!" Anita shuddered.

Helen shrugged. "I suppose it's some kind of tribal mark," she suggested. "It does make them look pretty fearsome, but I hardly notice it now. The Island people are some of the nicest there are. You mustn't be frightened of them."

"I'll try not to be," Anita agreed meekly. "But I do hope that I don't see them very often!"

"You'll have to see Taine-Mal fairly often," Helen told her dryly. "He keeps the boat supplied and you'll be getting the supplies from the hotel. In fact you'll have to work with him—"

"I'll try," Anita said immediately. "I will try, Helen. Only I've never had to earn my own living before. You will help me, won't you?"

"Of course I will, dear!" Helen agreed willingly. "It will be quite easy, you'll see. Besides, you'll like Peter Harmon—he's the manager of the hotel—and he'll help you with anything you don't understand."

"Was it he I spoke to on the telephone?" Anita asked timidly.

"That's right," Helen nodded.

"He's an American," Anita muttered, without enthusiasm. "I could tell by his accent!"

"It's an American hotel!" Helen said carefully, her patience fast evaporating.

"Mother——" Anita began, and then she stopped, blushing faintly at the expression on Helen's face. "I'm sorry," she said unhappily. "Only I lived with her for such a long time and one gets into bad habits!"

And of course Michael's mother didn't like Americans, Helen remembered. But then whom did she like? she asked herself with wry humour.

Na-Tinn's fleshy legs appeared at the top of the companionway. By bending nearly double, he could see them without coming down any further. He grinned awfully at Anita. "Feel better now?" he asked her with real concern. "Not good sailor, no? Never mind, land coming now!" He retreated up the stairs again, not expecting an answer, completely unaware of the quake he had left Anita in down below.

"Was that the same one?" Anita quavered.

"His brother," Helen grinned. Really she couldn't help laughing at Anita's expression. "It won't be much longer now!"

They came in to the jetty so quietly that down below they were hardly aware that they had arrived. It was only the blocking out of the portholes on the port side that told them they had come alongside.

"Good," said Helen. "Now we can get you to the hotel and get a good meal inside you! I expect you're tired after all this travelling?"

Anita nodded wearily. "I am tired," she admitted.

76

"I expect it's all the excitement of coming out of hospital and then coming straight here. But I'm all right, truly I am!"

Helen went up on deck first. She was delighted to see Miss Corrigan's comfortable figure on the jetty, her legs stiffly apart as she tried to keep her balance on the gimcrack erection which was swaying back and forth as the Polynesians jumped up and down on it, tying up the *Sweet Promise* and throwing ashore the used cylinders of compressed air, to be replenished before morning.

"Where's Anita?" Miss Corrigan called out immediately.

"She's here," Helen answered her. She stood aside so that the old lady would be able to glimpse Anita behind her. "How kind of you to come and meet her," she said as she jumped down on to the jetty.

"Not kindness at all," Miss Corrigan contradicted her. "It's because I'm a curious old hag! I couldn't wait to see her for myself. After all, we shall all be living in the same building, so we need to get along well together."

Anita shook hands with Miss Corrigan demurely. She had taken advantage of the extra minute she had spent in the saloon to run a comb through her hair and to set her hat back on her head at the same jaunty angle she had had it earlier. "Miss Corrigan," she breathed, "I'm so delighted to meet you. Helen says that you knew her father."

"Knew him well!" Miss Corrigan agreed. "You're a great deal prettier than I expected," she added, her obvious delight in the other's good looks softening the personal nature of the remark. "Are you fully recovered from your time in New Zealand? Helen was very worried about you."

"Yes, I'm quite recovered," Anita assured her. "Really, one is much better off without one's appendix, don't you think? It was a long trip today, though, and I must admit I'm exhausted after crossing that little piece of sea!"

"She was sick!" Gregory called down from the deck of the *Sweet Promise*. "She'll get over it with a bit of practice!"

"Oh no!" Anita cried out. "Never again! I couldn't!"

"You won't have to!" Helen said protectively. "Your job is to see to the supplies. It's mine to go on the *Sweet Promise*—"

"She'll love it if she comes with us once or twice," Gregory said loftily from his perch above them. "Almost everyone is seasick at first."

"Let me tell you that *nothing* would induce me to go on board that boat again! Not willingly anyhow!"

He grinned at her. "You'll change your mind!" he assured her cheerfully. "I'll come and look you up at the hotel, okay?"

Anita nodded and waved cheerfully. Helen hesitated for a moment longer. She wondered if she ought to ask him again to go easily on her sister-in-law, to explain how nervous she was and how easy it was to fluster her, but she decided that she had better allow him to find out for himself. At least he seemed to like Anita as a person, which was more than she thought he did her. She, Helen, he only tolerated, she knew, seeing her as a useful member of his team, but not at all as an attractive woman to dally with when neither of them were on duty.

Miss Corrigan walked between the two girls as they made their way to the hotel. Her ample figure provided a dumpy contrast to their slimness, a contrast which possibly only she appreciated.

"This is my village," she told them with pride, as they walked through the plaited palm huts of the fishermen. "I come here often. They are an interesting people, you know. When you have time, I'll take you about and introduce you to the headman." She tucked her arms into theirs and gave them a squeeze. "What fun it is to have the two of you here!" she exclaimed.

Helen grinned at her, knowing exactly what she meant. "Do you ever get lonely, Miss Corrigan?" she asked her.

"*Never!*" the old lady affirmed immediately. "I never have! But it's still nice to have you two young things to talk to in the evenings. Now, what I shall do is arrange a party for you both. Yes, that's it! We'll have a party!"

Helen saw Anita's face crumble into near terror. "What kind of party?" she asked nervously.

The old lady looked surprised. "Why, a proper party!" she exclaimed. "I'll talk to the headman about it tomorrow. We'll need flowers and enough coconuts to sink a ship! And roast sucking pig! The whole works! It *will* be fun! I can't wait to have it. I must consult Gregory as to when will be the best day. I don't suppose either of you have been here long enough to have a whole lot of social engagements to contend with, but with men one can never be quite sure, if you know what I mean!"

Helen blinked. "I wouldn't have thought there was much social life here!" she said.

Miss Corrigan chuckled. "Not at first sight," she agreed. "But Gregory is a great favourite with all the Islanders. They never have any occasion without asking him along as guest of honour. Surely Michael must have told you that!"

"No, he didn't," Helen said carefully.

"My brother was rather reserved about his doings here," Anita put in, choosing her words with a fierce concentration that made Helen laugh.

Miss Corrigan was at a loss. "Oh, dear," she said, "I've put my foot in it, haven't I? But I thought you must know because Michael went with Gregory so often. He was a great one for parties, that boy!"

Helen didn't like to admit that she knew less about

her husband than Miss Corrigan did, so she said nothing. She was glad when they reached the hotel and Miss Corrigan left them in the foyer to find their own rooms, saying that she would get Peter to put on something special for their evening meal. "We must make Anita feel welcome, mustn't we?" She hesitated. "You don't mind my calling you that, do you?"

Anita shook her head. "I've never been called anything else," she affirmed.

Miss Corrigan shook her head sadly. "My name is Ethel," she offered.

Both girls stood tongue-tied and awkward, abashed at the idea of using the old lady's given name. "We'll see you at dinner," Helen forced herself to say quickly. "We'll look forward to it."

"Yes," the old lady agreed, "if Anita isn't too tired. It's been a long day for her."

The lift bore them rapidly upwards to the landing where their rooms were situated. When the automatic doors opened, Helen stepped out first and led the way into Anita's room. It was exactly the same as her own, though the view was slightly different. From these windows it was possible to see the long lines of palm trees and the young men climbing them to bring down the coconuts and the wide, shady leaves if anyone had need of them. Nearer, almost directly beneath the windows, was a family of pigs, rooting through the undergrowth, grunting and squealing as they went.

"Do you like it?" Helen asked Anita.

Anita smiled and Helen was immediately aware of how seldom she had seen her smile at all before. It changed the whole expression on her face, giving a pretty tilt to her mouth and showing her fine, even teeth. "I love it!" she exclaimed. "Oh, Helen, I can't tell you how happy I am to be here!"

Helen helped her to unpack, keeping an eye on her as she did so. She could detect no particular sign of fatigue in Anita's face and she marvelled at how quickly one could recover from an operation in these days of marvellous new anaesthetics and modern methods of surgery. Just by looking at Anita, it was hard to believe that she had been in hospital at all.

"Miss Corrigan will be waiting for us," she said at last, when Anita had changed her dress and had unpacked everything else that she had brought with her.

Anita made a face. "Do we have to eat with her?" she asked. "I mean, do we have to every night? She's a quaint old thing, but I was rather hoping we could be by ourselves."

Helen turned from looking out of the window. "I think she'd be hurt if we didn't. She's nice. My father liked her very much and I think I do too."

Anita shrugged her shoulders. "Oh well, if your father liked her—" she said bitterly. She tensed suddenly. "What was your father doing out here?" she demanded.

"He came here before the war," Helen answered simply. "He was interested in the habits of sharks. They had several bad scares in the Islands, one or two people had been taken by sharks from quite close in, and so the Government sent for my father. I don't know what he did about it exactly, but he probably gave them some advice and it worked. Anyway, he met Miss Corrigan and they did a survey on the local fishing customs. They kept up a long and rather boring correspondence ever afterwards!"

Anita looked astonished. "And didn't your mother mind?" she asked.

"It wasn't that kind of relationship," Helen said dryly. "Miss Corrigan was old enough to be his mother!"

"Oh—oh, I see!" Anita laughed. "I hadn't

81

thought of that. I know so little about your family really. You don't mind my asking, do you?"

Helen reassured her with a smile. "Why should I?" she said.

But the knowledge that Miss Corrigan had once collaborated with her father did not seem to have raised her status much in Anita's eyes. She was kind and she was patient whenever the old lady was speaking, but she showed no signs of wanting to converse with her herself. On the contrary, she soon relapsed into silence, only addressing the occasional remark when it was absolutely necessary to Helen, but otherwise saying nothing at all. Helen hoped that Miss Corrigan had not noticed. She made a valiant attempt at keeping the conversation going while they sipped their drinks out on the terrace. Once or twice she caught Miss Corrigan's twinkly gaze resting on her and roused herself to think of yet more things to say. She could have wished, she thought, that Miss Corrigan herself would make a greater effort, but the old lady only sat back in her chair and watched the two girls from behind her drink, occasionally smiling to herself as if she possessed some private joke which was amusing her very much.

"I can tell Anita is Michael's sister," she said to Helen quite suddenly, when Anita had gone inside to fetch herself some insect repellant in a vain attempt to protect herself from the hundred and one flying insects that dive-bombed the lights and had a particular delight in biting or stinging her fair, pale flesh. "She has the same surface charm. Not so well developed as her brother's, but then I don't suppose she's had the same practice."

Helen stirred uncomfortably, making her chair creak in her embarrassment. "She's a very shy person," she said tentatively.

"Nonsense, my dear," the old lady said roundly. "How could she be shy at her age? I suspect you know more about shyness than she does! It will be interesting, though, to see what she turns into away from her mother."

It seemed to Helen that she might just as well have been discussing a caterpillar and what kind of butterfly it would become. "I'm very fond of Anita," she said crossly.

"Oh, quite!" Miss Corrigan agreed vaguely. Her eyes lit up as Peter Harmon came out on to the terrace to join them, carrying the evening's menu in his hand. "Peter," she greeted him, "come and join us and meet the new arrival!"

The American smiled and nodded. He drew up a chair and sat on the edge of it, ill at ease and without much hope of anything else. "She has arrived, then?" he said.

Anita came back on to the terrace, her eyes widening as she saw Peter. Watching her, Helen saw her hesitate and gather herself together. How strange, she thought, that anyone's facial expression could change so completely in a few seconds. And yet it had. Gone was the tired patience with which Anita had endured Miss Corrigan; now there was only interest and a faint, becoming colour that came and went as easily as she breathed.

"My, you must be Mr. Harmon?" she said, excitement bubbling through her voice.

"That's right, ma'am," Peter agreed. He held out his hand and swallowed nervously. "I hope you will be comfortable here," he added professionally.

Helen's eyes strayed to Miss Corrigan who was looking over her shoulder at the French windows that led out on to the terrace. She was surprised to see Gregory sauntering out towards them, immaculately dressed in a dinner jacket and black tie. He bowed slightly towards Helen, pointing down at his neatly polished shoes, and then he gave all his attention to Miss Corrigan, lightly kissing her on the hand.

"Well, as you can see, I came," he smiled down at her.

Miss Corrigan grunted witth satisfaction. "So I should hope!" she told him gruffly. "As a reward you can take Helen in to dinner!"

Gregory sat down easily on the nearest chair, grinning at all of them. "I can see we're all set for a truly civilised evening!" he said lightly.

Miss Corrigan reached out and slapped him on the knee. "Hush!" she said. "It doesn't do you any harm to dress properly now and then." She smiled with a sudden, flirtatious charm that was oddly appealing. "Don't you want to set our hearts a-quiver?"

Helen liked the way he immediately responded to the old lady, but then charm was not something that Gregory had ever lacked for any female.

"I'm flattered, Ethel," he murmured, and he looked it. "I'm really flattered. I didn't think you'd noticed I've been sweet-talking you ever since I got here!"

The old lady crowed with pleasure. "Get along with you!" she said. "You can save that sort of remark for those young enough to enjoy it!"

Gregory leaned right forward, still smiling lazily at her. "That's why I picked you," he told her. "Didn't you know?"

Helen was shocked to find that her hands were clenched in her lap. Why, she thought, she was downright jealous! But then she remembered that she knew all about charm and despised it. Michael had been charming. Surely she wasn't going to be bluffed a second time. If anyone knew that charm was skin deep and not worth considering, surely it was she!

# CHAPTER SIX

ANITA was still asleep when Helen tore herself out
of bed and began to get ready for the day's work
ahead of her. It had been a wonderful evening. Peter
had excelled himself by finding a number of local
dishes for them to sample and approve. He had
refused to serve turtle soup, but he had agreed to
using their eggs. They had tasted stronger than any
other egg Helen had ever had and were enclosed in
leathery, rather brittle shells. A single turtle would
lay many, many eggs in a season. The dangerous
time for the turtle was when they hatched out and
the minute turtles made their first dash for the sea.
Then they were the prey of every passing bird and
often of the islanders too who had a fancy for them.
Miss Corrigan had told them all about them. There
had been pineapples too, yams and asparagus, and
quite a number of things Helen had been unable to
put a name to. She had enjoyed them all, though,
just as she had enjoyed the impromptu dance afterwards.

Gregory had danced with all three of them in
turn. It might have been Helen's fancy that he had
been more formal with her than he had been with
Anita, but it was certain that the only time he had
really relaxed had been with Miss Corrigan. And
how the old lady could dance! Why, *that* had put
both the younger girls in the shade! Helen grinned
at the memory. Seeing Miss Corrigan doing the
Charleston or the Black Bottom had been a sight she
wouldn't forget in a long, long time!

The Polynesian waiter served her with fresh orange
juice, eggs and bacon, and coffee, with a sleepy air

that told that he had been up late as well. Helen greeted him cheerfully and was pleased to note that his teeth were perfectly normal and had not been filed to suit any peculiar fashion.

"How you getting on out there?" he asked her as she sat down at the table.

"It will take time," Helen told him. "It's partly the angle of the ship. If we jolt her, she might fall off the ledge and be lost for ever, so we're having to be rather careful. But we'll get the gold, don't you worry!'

The waiter shrugged his ample shoulders. "I'm not worried," he said gently. "I had my gold many years ago. When I was small I went up the trees, but now I work for the hotel instead. Everything American and convenient. Much better!"

She joined in his laughter. "I should think it's much safer!" she said.

"Oh yes," he agreed. "Climbing the trees is a young man's work." He went into the kitchens, leaving her to finish her breakfast alone. She did so as quickly as possible and then got up to go, gathering her things together so that she could hold them in one hand as she sauntered through the village towards the jetty.

There was silence on the *Sweet Promise* when she got there. She jumped on board and went below to stow away her things. The saloon was in turmoil and the door that led into the first of the two small cabins firmly shut. Helen wondered whether she should try to sort out the papers that had been left all over the table. As far as she could see there was no kind of order to them, but it was unlike Gregory to leave chaos anywhere unless there was some purpose to it. She went up on deck once again and tried to find Na-Tinn and Maine-Tal, but there was no sign of either of them. At least, she thought, the thudding of her feet on the deck above his head ought to waken Gregory.

But when, a quarter of an hour later, there was still no sign of movement, Helen went down below again and hammered on the door that separated the cabins from the saloon.

"Hey!" she called out. "Gregory! Are you there! Where is everyone?"

There was no answer immediately, but then she heard Gregory's voice saying, "Shan't be a sec. Shove the coffee on, will you?"

Helen did as she was told, sitting primly on the edge of a seat as she watched the dark liquid come to the boil. When Gregory appeared a minute later, she was surprised to see him still in his pyjamas.

"What a night!" he grunted.

"It was quite pleasant," Helen agreed coldly.

"You don't know the half of it! *That* was just the beginning. Have you any idea what time I got to bed?"

Helen shook her head, a glimmer of a smile in her eyes. He looked so different when he was in need of a shave and his hair was standing on end.

"It couldn't have been more than an hour ago!" he grumbled. He plonked a couple of mugs on the table and poured the coffee into them. "I suppose the men aren't here yet either?" he yawned.

"No," Helen said.

He grinned at her. "You're full of disapproval this morning," he told her.

"Wouldn't you be?" she retorted sweetly. "Imagine how it would be if I overslept and wasn't ready to leave when you were? What a fuss you'd make! And it would all be because I was a woman!"

"Very likely!" he said sourly.

"Well then?" she challenged him.

"Well, I spent most of the night on the other side of the island," he explained wearily. "A fisherman was taken by a shark just outside the reef yesterday and his relatives want to get the shark. It's a matter of honour with them."

"I know," Helen said flatly.

He looked at her with renewed interest. "Ah yes," he said thoughtfully, "your father had to with that, didn't he?"

Helen nodded. "It was a part of his work. What are they doing to get the shark?"

"It's a family matter. The nearest male relative of the man taken has to get the shark. It's as simple as that." Gregory sighed. "His relatives all help him, of course."

Helen went white. "And Na-Tinn and Taine-Mal —?"

"Are close relations," Gregory said flatly.

"Ah," said Helen, "so that's what it has to do with you!"

Gregory smiled ruefully. "I'm their blood brother," he admitted. "So, you see, it has rather a lot to do with me."

"What are you going to do?" Helen asked him simply.

Gregory ran his fingers through his tousled hair. "Have another go later on." He laughed shortly. "They're using me for bait. It's a novel sensation, I must say!"

Helen's eyes widened. "As *bait*!" she repeated. "Surely not! What do you have to do?"

"Stand absolutely still!"

"Is that all?"

"It's all I do," he said ruefully. "Na-Tinn swims round with a harpoon that he made himself in one hand and Taine-Mal has a knife, I believe. I haven't actually seen it!"

Helen was more shaken then she liked to admit. "I suppose you have some shark repellent?" she asked too casually to be convincing.

"My dear girl, I'm the *bait*! The idea is that I should *attract* the monster, not repel him!"

Helen sighed, thinking back to the stories her father had told her of dealing with sharks all over the world. "Why don't you use a cage?" she said suddenly.

"You know," he said thoughtfully, "that's quite an idea. How about your cooking my breakfast while I get dressed and then we'll go across and see what can be done?"

"All right," Helen agreed.

He disappeared into the cabin. "You get better all the time!" he shouted at her, through the almost closed door.

"Thanks," she said dryly.

He stuck his head round the door and grinned at her. "Now, now, there's no need to get prickly. I wasn't referring to your sex for once! I really mean it, Helen Hastings. Man or woman, I'm glad to have you on board!"

Helen could feel herself blushing. A great wave of burning colour rose into her face and she turned away quickly before he could see it. What a fool he would think her! She was mad with herself, furious that she should be such a ninny! She was annoyed, too, that her hands shook ominously as she broke some eggs into a pan and scrambled them for his breakfast. It was something, though, that she had calmed down by the time he had finished dressing and she was sure that she looked quite normal when he slid into the seat opposite her and she piled the food on to his plate, watching carefully to see that she didn't spill any of it.

"If we had a cage," she went on, just as if he had said nothing at all, "you could put me in it as bait and then there would be three of you to fight the shark."

His eyes met hers and she could feel herself blushing again. "I don't think it would do," he told her. "It's a family matter."

Helen sat down, the saucepan still in her hand. "It's not just an idle offer," she said seriously. "If you can be a blood brother, I suppose there's no reason why I shouldn't be a blood sister, is there? The smell of blood will bring the shark quicker than anything else. My father always said that it was fatal to dive amongst sharks if you had so much as a scratch on you."

"Look," he said, "I hate to remind you of it, seeing that you are so touchy about it, but you are a woman. This is man's work."

She held her head up high. "Who said?" she demanded.

"I just said it!" he retorted.

She gave him such a hurt and bewildered look that his own expression softened. 'You can't bear to stay away from trouble, can you?"

"Something like that," she admitted. "I'm not being stupid. I've heard my father on the subject many times, you know. I probably know better than you do all the dangers and what has to be done."

"Could be," he agreed readily enough. "It isn't only that though to be considered. The whole thing is hallowed by tradition in the Islands. We can't interfere with that!"

"Why not?" she pleaded.

"Because it isn't what we're here for," he insisted.

She could see the justice of that. "All right," she said. "But I'm coming with you! I must be able to do something, surely?"

Gregory nodded his agreement. He was busy eating the eggs and toast she had prepared for him and he was more relaxed than she had ever seen him before. Lines of tiredness etched out his eyes in his face and she was surprised to notice one or two silver hairs at his temples. He looked too young to her to be going grey, but when she thought about his age, she realised that he must be in his late thirties. He could probably give her nearly ten years, she thought, not without pleasure, and her a widow-woman with her married life behind her!

When he had finished, he went into his cabin to fetch his hat and an ancient harpoon that was was the only weapon he kept on board. Helen, when she saw it, dismissed it firmly as being quite useless, and so it was when she compared it to the sophisticated weapon her father had used.

"It's better than Na-Tinn's," Gregory told her cheerfully.

"I can't wait to see what his must be like!" she retorted dryly.

Gregory grinned. "It barely exists," he agreed. "But it's remarkable what they can do to a shark with the tools they have. There aren't many man-eaters which have got away."

And this one wouldn't! Helen knew that now. She could see the glint of determination in Gregory's eyes and she knew quite well, that although it was none of her business, the same light was shining in her own eyes. This was something she knew about, something that she could do, and nothing and nobody was going to stop her.

Gregory jumped down on to the jetty and turned to help her follow him. His touch on her arm was firm and did much to stop the sudden nervousness that had overtaken her. He smiled at her briefly. "I left the jeep beside the hotel. It's the best way of getting across the Island."

She nodded, not trusting her voice not to break if she said anything. The village, as they passed through it, was not the friendly place of yesterday, or even of that morning. The children stood in groups watching Gregory as he strode through the huts towards the hotel. They huddled together in search of comfort and it was obvious that the news of the shark had just reached them. It was a matter for the whole Island. Their whole lives were spent in and out of the sea that surrounded their homes. If one of them was taken by a shark, they knew they were all in danger. There was no other way, once a shark had tasted blood he had to die, and they had their own way of going about such things. All of them knew that Na-Tinn and Taine-Mal were the next of kin to the man who had been killed and that Gregory was their blood brother. Awed and frightened, they watched him pass between them, knowing the battle that was to come.

Helen shivered as they climbed into the jeep. "Cold?" Gregory asked her. She shook her head. 'Someone walking over my grave," she said lightly.

He looked at her long and seriously. "Sure you want to come?"

She shrugged her shoulders. "Just you try and keep me away!" she said impulsively.

He grinned. "I wouldn't dream of it," he answered mildly. "Not if you're set on it."

"I'm set on it," she assured him.

It was the first time that Helen had been right across the Island. She was surprised by the variation of vegetation that they passed through. In the centre of the Island, there were quite a number of small farms, with pigs rooting through the scrubby trees and shabby dogs lazing in the hot sun. The palm trees, with their valuable crop, edged the Island, but didn't really come very far inshore. Beneath them were a few giant tortoises that must have seen many hundreds of years to have have achieved such a size. They staggered forward a few steps and then rested, summoning their strength for the next few feet. Above them exotic birds, dressed in green and lemon yellow, shattered the silence with their hideous screams.

There were no proper roads. Tracks ran from one settlement to another, sometimes fading out in the middle of nowhere. Fortunately the jeep was well able to cut across the rough ground and the four-wheel drive made it less likely to get stuck in the shifting coral sand as they neared the coast on the other side of the Island.

Helen thought she had never seen anywhere so beautiful as the bay where they came out. The green water lapped gently the dead white sands and overhead the languid palm trees nodded gently in the breeze. A coral reef almost completely enclosed the bay, but where the two arms met, a deep channel led out to the ocean beyond. The water there looked dark blue, the water was so much deeper than in the shallows of the bay. It was there, Helen thought, that the shark had entered and had come and gone as he pleased ever since.

Gregory parked the jeep on the edge of the white sand and stepped down on to the tough strands of grass that was fighting for a living beneath the palm trees. At the sound of his footsteps a hundred small crabs darted back and forth across the beach and disappeared into quickly made holes, only to reappear as soon as the danger had passed. Helen scuffed her feet in the sand as they walked across it, a little afraid that a crab might take a grab at her toes, but they were far more scared than she was and ran, with that curious sideways motion which is unique to them, as fast as they could in the opposite direction.

Na-Tinn was waiting for them. He was seated in a dug-out canoe that had a rather fragile outride strapped on to the edge of the boat. With the help of a shaped plank of wood, he could make it go where he would, darting through the calm green water and stopping just as suddenly.

"It's still here, Boss," he addressed Gregory.

Gregory grunted. Some of the men had dropped a net across the entrance to the bay, but he knew that if the shark was determined to break out the net would not be much use. The channel was too deep. He stared in silence at the dark shape of the giant fish as it glided backwards and forwards across the bay. One black fin rose to the surface adding a touch of drama to the occasion. The men yelled and Na-Tinn waved his harpoon over his head, uttering some blood-curdling incantation as he did so.

"Well, what do you think?" Gregory said to Helen.

"I still think the cage is the best bet," she answered thoughtfully.

He nodded. He waved to Na-Tinn to come ashore and explained what they were going to do.

None of the Polynesians were happy with the idea. They had always dealt with sharks in the same old way, with one of them as bait and the rest of the family as hunters. It was a personal thing between the shark and themselves. There was a demon in the shark and there was an age-old ritual for gaining power over that demon. Who knew if the new way would be as effective? Who knew if the demon would be appeased, or if he would go straight into another shark and then there would be another death, perhaps another after that? Could they take the risk? "You are our blood brother," they protested to Gregory.

"That is why I am going to help you," he replied imperturbably. "We tried the other way for most of the night, didn't we?"

The crowd that had gathered at the edge of the sand muttered amongst themselves and, for a moment, Helen thought they were going to refuse to make the cage that Gregory was asking for. But there was an old man there who could remember that once before, a long time before, they had dealt with sharks by using a cage. His tired eyes surveyed Gregory with the calm of old age and then fell on

Helen. He pointed at her excitedly and she nodded, grasping his hands in greeting.

"He must remember my father!" she exclaimed.

"Very likely," Gregory agreed. He talked to the old man and the old one grinned at Helen. In a few minutes the men had started to make the cage, binding bamboo sticks together with twine. At best it was a rather ramshackle affair, but Helen thought that it would serve its purpose and give the shark something to tangle with before it reached the bait inside. She had few illusions however at what the shark could do with its wicked jaws and the shattering blows it could deliver with its tail. No cage would last long if the shark had other ideas.

"I wish you'd let me be the bait," she sighed to Gregory. "I'd feel a great deal happier if you were around with a harpoon in your hand!"

Taine-Mai heard her and grinned. He turned quickly to his brother, but Na-Tinn was adamant. "It's a family matter!" he insisted.

"I told you so!" Gregory said in an undertone to Helen.

"If you can become a member of the family, I don't see why I shouldn't!" she retorted.

The Polynesian men had a lengthy discussion while they were finishing making the cage. Helen couldn't understand a word of what they were saying, but she did understand the sideways looks they gave her, considering her proposal and what it would mean.

"It looks as though you've persuaded them," Gregory said to her. "Sure you want to go through with it? There's still time to change your mind!"

"I'm quite sure," she said seriously.

The men nodded their agreement. "You must be family," Na-Tinn told her.

Helen nodded. She didn't mind the prick in her wrist. She had her eyes tight shut and was hardly aware of when they did it. When she opened them again, she was surprised that it was Gregory who was standing beside her, and Gregory's wrist that they bound close against hers so that their blood would mingle, joining them together for all time. The place where they had cut her smarted for a few seconds and then they cut her loose.

"You now family," Na-Tinn said with satisfaction.

Helen flexed her fingers to restore her circulation. They had tied her very tightly to Gregory and she had pins and needles in her hand. "I'm glad," she smiled at them.

"I never thought to have you as my sister," Gregory commented, an amused smile hovering round his lips.

"I hadn't thought to have a brother either!" she retorted.

"Don't take advantage of my brotherly feelings," he warned her. "I'm still your employer, don't forget."

"As if I could!" she answered demurely.

He helped her into the cage. She was surprised to see that he was far more nervous than she. She had a strong urge to comfort him, to tell him that nothing was going to happen, but she was tongue-tied and stupid and couldn't think of anything to say that he might not misunderstand. Na-Tinn and Taine-Mal made a dash for the frail-looking outrigger canoes, pushing them out from the silver shore.

"We tow you out now," they told her.

She nodded, taking a deep breath as the water covered her limbs. Her wrist was smarting again and she couldn't help wondering if the smell of blood would reach the shark before they were ready. She tried to keep calm, to remember all the victorious stories her father had told her. No shark ever defeated him, she thought with pride. He had known their thinking processes and exactly how they would react in any given circumstance. But did she? Had she been right to

96

set such a trap with herself as the bait and only three men with outdated and almost useless harpoons to protect her?

The Polynesians let go of the ropes and she trod water gently, surveying the world through the bamboo bars that protected her. Na-Tinn held his harpoon close in beside him, his eyes flicking here and there across the water. Taine-Mal slipped overboard into the water, his knife gleaming and ready to do battle. But where was Gregory? Helen felt a moment's panic when she couldn't see him. She turned and twisted in the water, searching for him, only to find him close beside her, his harpoon firmly grasped in his hand.

"Are you sure that thing works?" she asked him with a marked lack of confidence.

"It works!" he reassured her. "Look out now, it's over there on your left!"

She glanced where he was pointing, marvelling at his calmness. "It's coming pretty close," she whispered.

"Isn't that the idea?" he answered in such normal tones that she was ashamed of her own fears.

"Well, of course it is!" she said rather heartily. She dropped down under the water, opening her eyes and trying to adjust to the green haze of the water. She could make out the giant dark shape of the shark quite well, coming closer and closer even while she watched. Its great snapping jaws made her shiver and she was suddenly concerned, not for herself, but for Gregory, swimming so closely beside her and without the protection of the cage.

She surfaced and flipped her wet hair back out of her eyes. "Why doesn't Na-Tinn attack?" she cried out. "If he lets it get much closer it'll be too late!"

"Hush up now," Gregory said grimly, all his concentration directed on the great fish of the sea. He signalled with his hand to Na-Tinn to come in closer, until the shark had to swim between them to get to the cage. Taine-Mal stood up in his fragile craft, ready to dive in and help finish off the beast.

Helen heard the crack of the harpoon being fired and the whirring of the rope as it sprang through the air. It caught the shark amidships and its great tail thrashed the water as it tried to escape. A second later Na-Tinn had released his harpoon also, but it missed the writhing fish and hit the edge of the cage just beside where Helen was treading water, moving as little as she could to disturb their aim. She heard the Polynesian swear and recoil the rope as fast as he could. He would never make it in time, she knew that! The great fish was coming nearer and nearer. With one sweep of its mighty tail it could break up the cage and she had nothing with which to protect to herself. She prayed that Gregory would be able to hold it away from her, but the harpoon was so old and inadequate that she doubted it.

She didn't see Taine-Mal go into battle with his knife in his hand, reaching down to the belly of the shark and stabbing it with vicious strokes. She did see the shark turn and snap at its new attacker and then a new danger presented itself. She was horrified to see that Gregory had turned his back on the proceedings, hanging on to the harpoon with all his might. Another few inches and the shark's jaws would reach him.

"Look out!" she shouted vainly, knowing that he couldn't hear her. She rattled the bamboo bars of her cage to try and distract the shark, but she was too late. Gregory received a great gash down the whole length of his leg and she could see his blood flowing freely into the water. He let go of the harpoon just as the shark snapped at him again, but this time the fish was too slow. Taine-Mal slit its throat as it turned, keeping below the fish the whole time, and in that second Na-Tinn released his harpoon a second time and dragged the dying fish away from Gregory, away from the cage, and into the shallows where his family were waiting.

Helen broke out of the cage with her bare hands. She was oblivious of the scratches she received from the rough bamboo. Her only care was to reach Gregory as quickly as she could. He was hurt, for all she knew he was dying, and she was completely helpless, being kept from him by a barrier of her own contriving. When she had broken free, Taine-Mal had already taken Gregory into his canoe and was looking with horror at the long, angry wound that ran right down his thigh and leg.

Helen swam to the canoe and pulled herself level with Gregory's ashen face. "It'll need a few stitches," he said faintly. "Did we get him?"

She nodded, quite unable to speak. It would be weeks before Gregory's leg would be well enough for him to dive again. She looked at the long gash, feeling rather sick.

"We'll have to get you to a doctor," she said.

Taine-Mal nodded. "Plenty good doctor waiting on sand," he told her cheerfully. "Boss be quite all right, you see!" He grinned cheerfully. "Got shark!" he added joyfully. "Plenty celebration tonight!"

But Helen was beyond caring about the shark. She helped to ease Gregory out of the canoe and on to the fine white sand. She was terrified that the powdered coral would get into the wound and turn it septic. She had visions of him losing his leg and was horrified to find that she was crying.

The doctor was quite unlike any other doctor she had ever seen. He was dressed in no more than a tribal skirt, with his chest and arms naked and as smooth as a woman's. He sat down cross-legged beside his patient and prepared an injection which he unceremoniously plunged into Gregory's thigh. Helen watched him threading a needle as calmly as if he were seated in a European hospital with every facility at his command

and gritted her teeth to keep back the protests that rose unbidden to her lips.

"Is it painful?" she asked, her voice hoarse with emotion.

The doctor grinned cheerfully at her. "Not painful, no!" he laughed. "Not painful at all! Look, Mr. de Vaux has fainted!"

Helen swallowed, scared that she too would pass out, and the doctor began the lengthy task of sewing up the long wound as casually as if he were sewing up a rent in a pair of trousers.

# CHAPTER SEVEN

"HE'S a mighty skinny-looking fellow, but he'll live!" said the doctor.

Helen was shocked. "Skinny?" she repeated.

The doctor grinned. "Can you drive the jeep?" he asked her. "You'd better get him settled in at the hotel before he comes round. That leg'll pain him for a day or two yet."

"Skinny!" Helen said again.

"So he is!" the doctor said again. "Now, look at any Polynesian and you'll see what a man ought to look like. When he sits on the ground, he should rise up from it like a mountain with his head at the peak. He's skinny!" He said it with wry affection, carefully easing Gregory's unconscious form into the back of the jeep.

Certainly the doctor filled out his own prescription, Helen thought. He was a mountain of a man all right! His thighs were enormous and his whole body was thick and soft. Only his face held a touch of austerity, his black eyes flickering intelligently behind yet more rolls of fat.

"I wish the road were better," Helen sighed.

The doctor nodded. "I'll sit in the back and hold him," he said.

"And the shark?" Na-Tinn interrupted suddenly. "You must take the shark back with you. Missie Corrigan will need for party!"

Helen would have refused to take the monstrous fish. Even now, when it was dead and still, she was afraid if its great jaws. But her word counted for nothing in the face of their exuberant whoops of joy as they loaded the shark on to the passenger seat beside her, head downwards and with its great tail waving backwards and forwards as they jolted along the tracks that served for roads on the Island. If it fell out, Helen thought, she wouldn't be able to bring herself to touch it. She disliked everything about it, including its colour.

"Gently now, he's coming round," the doctor warned her.

Helen slowed almost to a stop, glancing over her shoulder at Gregory. He looked very ill to her. His face was the colour of putty and his normally firm face was slack. The sight of him smote her like a physical blow. Why should she care so much? But she did, so it was no good going on about it, she chided herself. Now was the time for her to be calm and collected and to make things as easy as she could for him.

She gritted her teeth. "It isn't far now," she said.

The smell of the shark beside her was strong and unpleasant. It was curious, she thought, how all species had their own distinctive smell and how one grew used to the ones that surrounded one all the time and was easily revolted by those which were strange. She half-hoped that the shark would fall out of the jeep and leave her in peace, but it had been wedged in too securely. Only the tail waved to and fro as they travelled on across the Island and just occasionally it came so close to her head that she could feel it against her hair. She shivered. She was beginning to be obsessed by the shark's grim, grinning face, and the putty look on Gregory's. The doctor looked barely competent to her. She just hoped that he knew what he was doing, moving Gregory at all! Though what else he could have done, she couldn't have said.

The hotel looked large and familiar and comfortably Western. When it came in sight, Helen unconsciously relaxed. She put her foot down hard on the accelerator and the jeep shot forward the last few yards down the road towards the only skyscraper that the Islands could boast.

Miss Corrigan came running out of the hotel, almost as if she had been watching for their arrival. Her eyes fell immediately on the shark. "Oh, it's a big one!" she said ecstatically. "*Just* the thing for my party!"

Helen forbore to say that she for one would be quite unable to eat a single bite of the loathsome fish. "Gregory is hurt," she said.

Miss Corrigan peered through her short-sighted eyes into the jeep. When she saw Gregory's leg her gasp was quite audible. "The poor boy!" she exclaimed. "The poor boy! We must get him inside at once." Her hand rested for an instant on the doctor's naked shoulder. "I'm so glad you were there," she said with real feeling. "The poor boy!"

The doctor grinned, revealing fine even teeth. "He'll do now he's in your care!" he told her. "I suppose the hotel has a room?"

Miss Corrigan laughed. "How can you ask? You must know that it's still empty except for us! That's naughty of you!"

The doctor shrugged. "I thought perhaps the American tourists had arrived," he said, far too innocently. "They are expected, aren't they?"

"Sooner or later!" Miss Corrigan brushed the remark aside. "I'll fetch Peter."

Peter Harmon arrived white of face and extremely concerned. "Is he hurt real bad?" he asked. "I wonder if we have the facilities here. Should I arrange to have him flown out?"

"Certainly not!" Miss Corrigan squashed the idea flat. "He has Helen and me to nurse him—Anita too, come to that! And the doctor will be on hand!"

Peter looked at the long wound and shuddered. "He'll have a scar for life!"

"At least he'll have his leg to walk on," the doctor drawled. "Shall we get him inside?"

Helen steeled herself to taking a good at the gash on Gregory's leg herself. She would have to get used to it, she told herself. This was not the time to be squeamish. That would do nobody any good. She was surprised to discover that Gregory was conscious again, his eyes fixed on the shark's tail in front of him.

"Gregory?" Helen said uncertainly.

He conjured up a smile. "Don't looked so mazed, Helen," he chided her. "It doesn't suit you!"

"But —"

"But your plan worked, didn't it? Isn't that the shark I see before me?"

It had been her idea, of course, but Helen couldn't help wishing that he wouldn't remind her of the fact. It hadn't been a part of it that anybody would be hurt, but in justice to herself she had to admit that it might have been worse, if she had not been there someone might have been killed.

"Yes, it worked," she said slowly.

"Well then, what is there to look so down in the mouth about?"

She smiled uncertainly. "Well, if you don't know I certainly don't," she retorted.

It was a long, painful business getting Gregory into the hotel all the same. In the end Peter practically carried him single-handed, with the doctor following behind, a benign expression on his face and with his doctor's bag in his hand. They had travelled painfully through the foyer towards the lift, when the doors suddenly clanged open and there was Anita standing before them, as astonished to see them as they were to see her.

"What happened? Oh, Helen, how could you let this happen?" she demanded and, to Helen's dismay, her eyes filled with tears and her mouth trembled ominously.

"We're trying to get him to bed," Helen said patiently, hoping that Anita would hurry out of the lift and allow them to enter.

"You did it!" her sister-in-law said flatly. "I suppose Michael dying wasn't enough for you?"

Miss Corrigan was shocked. "What nonsense!" she said gruffly. "Here, girl, get out of our way!"

Anita obligingly moved. "Will he be all right?" she asked abruptly.

"Of course," the doctor said gently. "He is in my care!"

Gregory himself said nothing. He looked exhausted. Helen wept inwardly for him. If only they could get him into bed, where he could rest and sleep awhile, then perhaps he would feel a bit better. It was obvious that he was nearing the end of what he could endure in the way of pain and discomfort. She thought that she couldn't bear it if he lapsed into unconsciousness again. He didn't. Once in the lift, he seemed to recover a little.

"It will be strange to sleep on land for a change," he said with a wistful touch of humour.

"Sleep," the doctor nodded approvingly. "More sleep the better!"

They got him out of the lift, with Peter taking most of the strain, and into one of the empty bedrooms just across the corridor. Helen looked round the room curiously, expecting it to be like the ones allotted to her and Anita, but this one was quite different. There was none of the glamour and none of the South Seas atmosphere that characterised their rooms. This one was sparsely furnished, with rugs on the floor and thinner rugs covering the bed. There were no pictures on the wall and mighty little in the way of a view from the window.

"It isn't our best room," Peter said apologetically. "But it's convenient. You'll need a bit of nursing and the girls can get in and out from you here without any difficulty."

"It looks grand to me," Gregory answered thankfully. "Thanks for taking me in."

Peter looked at him, embarrassed. "It's nothing," he muttered. "Hadn't you better get into bed?"

"Yes," Helen said firmly. "The sooner you're in bed the better. I'll leave you to it."

In the corridor she met Anita, slightly puffed from running up the stairs. "Oh, Helen, you must tell me all about it! Poor Gregory! Doesn't he look ill?" Her chin trembled. "I suppose he is all right?" she sighed.

"There's nothing to tell," Helen said abruptly. She thought Anita was going to cry, but she didn't. Instead, she looked very brave and feminine and made Helen feel quite uncomfortably unconcerned and indifferent to human suffering. "Do you want to see the shark?"

Anita shuddered. "*The* shark?"

Helen nodded. "They thought Miss Corrigan would want it for her party. It's in the jeep."

"I think that's horrible!" Anita burst out. "And I think you're horrible too! You don't care that Gregory is hurt, do you? Not really! You'll be telling me next that it's a pity because it will put the diving schedules back still more, or something like that!"

Helen's face twisted into a smile. "I hadn't thought of that," she said bleakly. "I rather wish you hadn't reminded me."

"Well, I'm not!" Anita retorted. "You'd have thought of it sooner or later!"

"I might have done," Helen agreed mildly, "but how I hope that Gregory has not!"

That was a forlorn hope, however. When she and Anita were called into Gregory's room, she knew immediately, by the lines of anxiety around his mouth, that he too had been made aware of how long it was going to be before he did any more diving.

"It's been a pretty disastrous expedition one way and another," he said bitterly.

"Don't worry about it," Helen said immediately. "I'll manage somehow!"

He smiled at her. "You don't know your own limitations, woman. Did anyone ever tell you that?"

"Often," she admitted.

Anita pressed her knees against the side of the bed and leaned consolingly over Gregory's prone body. "You mustn't worry," she said anxiously.

"That's easier said than done," he told her wryly.

"No, it isn't really," she contradicted him. "You don't know what Helen is really like. She'll probably manage better without you than if you were there. She'll manage everything, just you see!"

Helen blushed. "Anita!" she exclaimed helplessly.

Gregory frowned. "It's nice to know that I'm an optional extra to my own plans!" he said dryly.

"But you're not!" Helen interposed hastily, aware in the pit of her stomach that the damage was already done. "We'll just have to hold up proceedings until you're better."

"I can't afford to do that either," he said crossly. "If anyone should know that, it's you!"

There would be no pleasing him now, she knew that, but Helen felt she had to try all the same. The grey look was back on his face and she would have done anything to dispel that. "Perhaps you can tell me exactly what to do from your bed," she suggested. "I can't manage otherwise!"

Anita's eyes flickered over her anxious face. "You've got the Polynesian sailors to help you, haven't you? Why do you have to bother Mr. de Vaux?"

"Why indeed?" Gregory sighed. He eased himself against his pillows. "For heaven's sake let the subject drop now, will you? I can't think straight at all. I wish you hadn't brought it up, Helen—"

"I didn't!" she protested.

"Oh, God!" he said irritably. "Must we have an argument about everything?"

Helen bit her lip. "No," she said.

"Why don't you go now?" Anita whispered to her. "I'll look after Mr. de Vaux"

She was probably right, Helen thought diffidently. She gazed helplessly at Gregory, but he was not interested in anything further that she might have to say. She thought she would remember for ever how tenderly Anita hung over his bed and just how he looked in a pair of Peter's pyjamas which were far too small for him. And yet what did she care if Anita was better for him at the moment? What was it to her? Gregory de Vaux was no more than her employer and one, moreover, who had been around when her husband had been killed! She would do well to remember that!

Miss Corrigan was sipping a cool drink out on the verandah. Helen noticed with amusement how straight she sat in her chair, despite her plump figure and eager manner.

"May I join you?" she asked her.

"Why, of course, dear! What will you have to drink? Where's that Anita of yours? Is she coming down too?"

Helen forced herself to look cheerful. "I think she's cheering up Gregory," she said. "She has a gentle approach that he likes."

Miss Corrigan blew noisily down her nostrils. "Nonsense!" she exclaimed finally. "I'll grant you she's a very feminine girl, but she'll annoy Gregory soon enough. That man is no fool, and there are mighty few that one can say that about!"

"At least she doesn't annoy him as much as I do," Helen sighed. "Miss Corrigan, do you mind if I ask you something? What are you going to do with the shark?"

Miss Corrigan smiled. "You'll see, at my party," she promised. "I'll have the teeth turned into a necklace for you."

Helen shivered. "I don't think I'd like that," she said. "I'd remember what those teeth did to Gregory every time I looked at them."

Miss Corrigan looked at her thoughtfully. "You'll be telling me next that you're in love with the man!" she said obliquely.

Helen blushed. "But that wouldn't be true!" she said in such a rush that the words ran into one another and she didn't think that the old lady had understood her properly. "How could you think such a thing? You forget! I'm only here because it was here that Michael died. I haven't any other reason to stay. You must be able to see that?"

Miss Corrigan laughed. "I see what I want to see, like everyone else," she said flatly. "Drink up, my dear, I have things to do."

The sun had only just risen above the horizon, casting a red and gold glow over the whole island, when Helen slipped on her clothes and started through the village towards the jetty and the *Sweet Promise*. Taine-Mal was already on board, though; as soon as he saw her, he came hurrying across the jetty, his usual cheerful grin stretched on his face. "Hullo, little sister, how are you now?" he greeted her.

Helen swallowed her amusement. "How are you?" she retorted.

His grin grew, revealing yet more filed teeth to her gaze. "I am happy now the shark is dead and my family is revenged," he said.

"You must be," she agreed sympathetically. "I'm afraid it wasn't quite such a successful operation as I had hoped," she sighed. "My father would have done much better."

"But our little sister understands these matters very well," he said with such obvious pride that she was touched. "The Boss said as much before he was hurt. The Boss like you very much."

Helen was afraid she would cry. "I think you are exaggerating," she said mildly. "Will you help me on board?"

He did so with a gentle touch that she found soothing balm to her bruised spirit. "I'm afraid that we won't get much diving done until Mr. de Vaux is better," she said to him.

"But you can dive," he replied, astonished.

'But can you and Na-Tinn manage the boat between you?" she asked him quickly.

This touched his professional pride. "Of course," he said simply.

Helen believed him. She went down below into the saloon in a thoughtful mood. Perhaps it would be possible, she thought. If she herself did the diving, the Polynesians were well trained when it came to looking after things above surface. Only she had never taken responsibility for a dive before. Supposing she couldn't find the ship? It was quite possible, for she knew nothing whatsoever about navigation. Slowly she unrolled the charts that she had seen Gregory use, wondering if she would be able to understand them. Lines and lines of little figures covered the white sheets and at first sight she thought they were going beyond her. But when she looked at them closer, she found that they were quite reasonable. She could follow the line of the reef and she could see exactly which parts were deep enough for her to be able to take the *Sweet Promise* through to where the wreck was lying.

"Taine-Mal!" she called up the companionway.

"Little sister!"

"Has Na-Tinn come on board yet?"

"Sure thing. He's patching the sails. The spare ones sure are a mess!"

Helen hesitated. "Could you ask him to come down here?" she said.

She shrugged her shoulders, knowing that she had already made her decision even if she was going to consult the others to see if they thought it was a possibility. She was going to take out the *Sweet Promise* and she was going down to the wreck by herself to lay the ship open ready for Gregory as soon as he was well enough to dive again.

Na-Tinn came down the steps and stood respectfully a few feet away from where she was standing, leaning over the table and frowning fiercely in an effort to concentrate on the charts better.

"Do you know anything about these charts?" she asked him abruptly.

He shook his head. "No, little sister. But they are not needed by us. I can take a boat anywhere in Melongese waters without trouble. I have always known these waters."

"In a small dug-out canoe perhaps," she said doubtfully. "But the *Sweet Promise* needs quite a bit of water under her."

Na-Tinn smiled gently. "I know the way to the wreck. I could find it blindfolded. Truly, little sister, I know these waters."

"I hope so." Her eyes met his. There was something about his warm confidence that convinced her. "Gregory would never forgive us if anything were to happen," she said.

"The Boss will be pleased," he answered. "Nothing bad will happen. It will be much worse if we lose the good time. The wreck may not stay on the reef for another season of rain and typhoons. The Boss won't be pleased if we lose everything that way."

"So we go," Helen said.

Na-Tinn nodded and grinned. "I go tell Taine-Mal," he said.

Actually it was easier than Helen had thought. Na-Tinn cast off the ropes fore and aft and she slipped the engine into gear, shoving her knee against the long shaft until it clicked into position. Slowly the *Sweet Promise* came about and chugged out of the harbour, through the narrow channel in the reef and out into the rougher waters beyond. Helen knew a moment of acute anxiety as the men hauled up the sails and the wind took over from the engine, speeding the *Sweet Promise* over the open sea. The spray came down on the deck like fine rain, smelling salt and clean. Behind, they left a wake that was straight and true and before them was the whole archipelago of islands, each looking prettier than the last, and each with its own reef of coral and small, calm bays edged with white sand and palm trees, looking like a paradise indeed.

Helen turned the wheel over to Na-Tinn and went forward to check the diving equipment. Nothing, absolutely nothing, could be allowed to go wrong. She checked and double checked each individual part and then, when she was satisfied, went below and changed into her diving suit. Taine-Mal helped her into the harness that carried the cylinders of compressed air and tied the weighted belt around her waist. Na-Tinn dropped the sails and the anchor chain gushed out of its holes and dropped deep down into the sea. The *Sweet Promise* came to a shuddering stop and sat, quivering, in the navy blue sea. A few feet away the colour of the water changed, pointing out where the shelf was down below. They had come to the right spot, Helen was sure of that. So far it was going well, she thought, and hoped earnestly that the rest of the day would be as good as its beginning.

The Polynesian brothers helped her over the side

and into the water. She took longer than usual to accustom herself to the water and to fit her mask to make sure that the air was flowing properly and that she was quite comfortable. When she was quite ready, she signalled up to them for the rest of the equipment and then struck out downwards towards the dim shape of the sunken frigate below her.

The list of the wreck had increased since she had last been down. She wasn't sure how she knew it, but she was quite sure that it had shifted. Her heart hammered within her as she moved round the shelf, changing her approach to the wreck so as to disturb it as little as possible. Beneath the bows of the frigate, she could see the crushed coral that was holding the wreck on to the shelf. There was no doubt that it was beginning to give way. She would have to hurry if she was going to open up a hole large enough for them to crawl inside before the shelf gave way entirely and the frigate sank down into the measureless depths below where they would never be able to reach her.

She soon found the place where they had been working before and started the lengthy business of burning her way through the outer plate. It wasn't long before the heavy metal gave way. Even in the water where weights are far less than they would be on land, it was as much as she could do to hold it away from the wreck and send it spinning down below. There was only the inner skin of the ship now to cut through and she set to work with a will, setting herself the task of doing a certain number of feet before she surfaced.

When she did surface, her oxygen gauge registered nearly empty. It was silly to take such a stupid risk, she told herself crossly, but even so a warm glow of satisfaction spread over her at the thought of how much she had achieved and quite by herself. By the time Gregory was well enough to dive, she would have opened up the side of the frigate and there would be nothing else to do before they went inside and brought up the gold.

Na-Tinn and Taine-Mal were as pleased as she was. "You tell the Boss about it tonight?" they asked her.

"I might do," she answered. She wasn't very sure that she would talk to him at all. If he still looked as grey and pale as he had the day before, he would be better off sleeping and resting rather than worrying about what she was doing. She wondered if Anita had whiled away the time with him all day and what they would have found to talk about. She wouldn't have thought that they would have had anything in common, but since coming to the Islands Anita had surprised her. Even so, if she hadn't seen her hanging over Gregory's bed for herself, she wouldn't have believed it of her sister-in-law. There had been nothing of the timid, self-effacing girl that she had always known in the look Anita had given Gregory then.

Helen refused to think about it any more. It was funny how her thoughts kept going back to that moment, but she wouldn't allow it. She would keep busy and think about other things. And that was exactly what she did all day. It was later than usual when they took the *Sweet Promise* back into the harbour and tied up at the jetty. The sun had set and it was as black as ink all about them. Taine-Mal lit a hurricane lamp and gave it to Helen to carry to light her way back to the hotel.

"You tell the Boss for us," he told her. "You tell him we carry on just fine!"

"Yes," Na-Tinn agreed. "You tell him, little sister."

Even so she might not have done, only when she got to the hotel, Miss Corrigan was there waiting for her.

"Where have you been, child?" she demanded loudly. "I wanted you to help me prepare for my party!"

"I took the *Sweet Promise* out," Helen told her.

"So Gregory thought," Miss Corrigan retorted, unmollified by the explanation. "You'd better go up and see him."

"Now?" Helen said wearily. "I was hoping to change and freshen up a bit."

"He's expecting you immediately," Miss Corrigan muttered relentlessly. "You should have told someone you were going!"

Gregory's door was shut. Helen hesitated outside, putting off the moment when she would have to knock go in. "Come in," Gregory's voice bade her briskly. He sounded positively robust to her anxious ears. Robust and quite strong enough to bawl her out if she gave him the chance. She opened the door and went inside, hoping that she looked rather more confident than she felt.

Gregory was sitting up in his bed. The grey look had gone from his face and he looked quite as well as she had ever seen him.

"Oh, you're better!" she said with real pleasure.

"Much better!" he agreed.

"I'm glad," she added awkwardly.

His eyes held hers mercilessly. "So you've taken out the *Sweet Promise* and brought her back —"

"Unscathed," she interrupted him quickly.

"Unscathed but *late*!" he retorted.

Helen said nothing. She thought that she must look a sight, with her hair all wet from the sea, and her face and hands unwashed and sunburned.

"How did the day go?" he asked more gently.

She told him that they were through the outer plate and that she had begun on the inner steel lining. He listened carefully to every word she said.

"Any shifting?" he asked then.

"A bit," she admitted.

His eyes met hers again. "I was afraid of that," he said. "Look, Helen, you're to promise me you won't attempt to go inside by yourself. Is that clear?"

She nodded. "Yes," she said.

He sighed with relief. "Then I don't mind telling you that my leg hurts like hell and it'll be a while before I can dive again." He grinned at her with real affection. "You're a better assistant than I deserve, Helen, my love!"

Helen swallowed, longing to make some light retort but finding nothing to say. Instead, she hurried out of the room and slammed the door shut behind her. At least, she thought, she was glad he was looking better.

# CHAPTER EIGHT

THE first group of American tourists was expected to arrive on the same day as Miss Corrigan's party. Peter Harmon had a theory that the local colour that the party could be expected to provide would do much to balance the unfortunate impression that he felt the swaying bamboo jetty and the other lack of facilities were bound to create.

"They would send them before we're ready!" Peter moaned. "I'm surprised they even allowed the plaster to dry out! What on earth do they expect me to do with them?"

"I don't suppose you'll have to do much," Helen tried to comfort him. "I expect most of them will want to lie on the gorgeous beaches and that will be about it!"

Peter grunted. "I shall have to move you out of your rooms, I'm afraid. Do you think Anita will mind?"

"Why should she?" Helen wondered.

Peter shrugged. "She's a might fussy that way," he remarked. "Haven't you discovered that?"

Helen was surprised. "You're imagining things," she told him. "Anita has never had anything much. Her mother saw to that!"

"Then she's making up for lost time," he said dryly.

Helen laughed. "I don't blame her for that!" Helen said quickly. "You should meet my revered mother-in-law! The only person who ever managed to catch her attention was my husband. I think she was fond of him in her own way, but poor Anita never had a scrap of affection from the old dragon."

Peter grinned "That's funny," he said. "She's made quite an impression here!"

Helen bit her lip. "With Gregory, you mean?"

"With us all," Peter answered her. "She's been about most of the time you've been out diving and she's done quite a bit of the nursing that Gregory needed." He smiled. "She's got quite an air about her, hasn't she?"

"Has she?" Helen said, astonished. "I can't say I've ever really noticed."

"She's put me in my place more than once," Peter reminisced with a thoughtful expression. "I'd say she was enjoying herself on the Melonga Islands. How about you?"

"I shall enjoy it better when Gregory gets back on his feet!" Helen sighed. "That reminds me, did Anita give you my shopping list for next week?"

"She's got it in hand," he answered indifferently. "As a matter of fact she put through my order as well while she was about it. One never knows what tourists are going to think they want." He cracked his knuckles thoughtfully. "I wonder if they even know that there's nothing here as yet!"

"There's me diving!" Helen protested.

A glint of appreciation came into his eyes. "I'll remember to tell the male members of the party," he promised.

"You do that!" said Helen. She was getting low in cylinders of compressed air and she wished that Peter had sent the order to Auckland so that she could be sure that it would arrive before Gregory was up and about and demanding to know where it was. It wasn't that she didn't trust Anita, but if she had known her sister-in-law was going to put in the order she would have checked it beforehand. Anita knew very little about such things and she showed remarkably few signs of wanting to increase her knowledge. It was yet another thing that was worrying Helen. Anita was being paid by Gregory, not by Peter, and as far as she could see Gregory was getting mighty little in return for his generosity.

"When do you want me to move my room?" she asked Peter.

He got up to go, checking his thoughts against the list he held in his hand. "As soon as you can," he said. "They'll be here the day after tomorrow!"

Gregory was the only one who didn't have to shift his room. It was just as well, for although he had only been in it a matter of days, it was completely chaotic. Well-wishers from all over the Islands had brought him gifts of shells, sharks' teeth, and special fruits and foods. Piles of treasures stood in every corner of the room, the most valuable being a collection of black pearls that he kept on the table beside his bed so that he could finger them whenever he wanted to and admire their iridescent beauty.

Helen had found it increasingly difficult to visit him. She could think of nothing to say once the subject of their work had been exhausted, and she had the feeling that she was unwelcome anyway. So she was surprised when, in the middle of moving her things to another bedroom on a different floor of the hotel, one of the Polynesian waiters came and found her.

"Mr. de Vaux want to speak with you," he told her. "If you have time now."

Helen knew that she would make time no matter how busy she was. She nodded briefly to the waiter and bundled her possessions into her new room in a hurry, racing down the stairs again because she couldn't be bothered to wait for the lift.

She was surprised, when Gregory bade her come in, to find him up and dressed.

"Do you think you ought to be up?" she asked him.

He smiled. "Why not? It's been a few days now, you know."

It was a relief to her, though quite how much of a relief she didn't want him to know. "Wh—what do you want?" she said instead.

He gave a slightly quizzical look. "Do I have to want anything?" he teased her.

"N—no," she agreed. "But Miss Corrigan and Anita seem to have done a very good job nursing you."

He made a face at her. "They were eager enough," he agreed with a touch of resentment. "It's not exactly an experience I want to repeat!"

Helen felt again the horror she had known when he had lain on the coral beach, looking grey and remarkably close to death. "I should hope not!" she said.

He smiled faintly. "The truth is that I'm bored stiff!" he told her. "I was hoping that you'd tell me all that you've been doing on the frigate?"

"I've made quite a hole in her!" she grinned.

"No trouble?"

"None so far. But she's rocking again." Some of the anxiety she had been feeling surfaced again into her mind. "There's no chance of any storms or anything until we've finished, is there?"

"I shouldn't think so," he answered soberly. "You did listen when I told you not to go inside on your own, didn't you?"

"I wouldn't dare!" she said frankly.

"Good. Now tell me exactly what you've done."

Helen sat down in the spare chair in his room and began. She found, to her surprise, that she was enjoying herself. She told him how her navigation was improving and how she had fitted up a radio contact between herself as diver and *Sweet Promise*.

"Does it work?" he asked her.

"More or less. It will be a great help when you can come out with us again. I think Na-Tinn is rather scared of my disembodied voice!"

She told him too of the turtle she had befriended. "I think it's a green turtle," she explained. "I've never seen such a monster. It gave me the fright of my life when it first came round the wreck, but I've got used

120

to it now. I don't know if it's male or female," she confessed with a laugh.

"You soon will," he told her. "The females make their nests ashore to lay their eggs. Turtles have reversed the process of evolution. They started on land and went into the sea. They have to be hatched out on land to be able to breathe. I'm afraid not many survive their first walk to the sea."

"Why not?" she asked, fascinated.

"The birds take them. There may be as many as a hundred eggs hatching out at a time and sometimes there isn't even one solitary survivor. I thought of trying to farm them at one time. It would be easy enough—and think of all the food they would provide. Anyway, I've never had the time. I did once save a few eggs and hatched them out right away from the birds, but even most of those were taken out of the sea when I released them. Somehow the birds seem to know by instinct where they are. But if one rigged up some netting and covered in one or two bays in that way, one would soon have more turtles than one would know what to do with!"

Helen's eyes shone with excitement. "I'd love to try it," she said.

"Okay, it's a date. As soon as we've finished the work in hand!"

She longed to be as enthusiastic as he was, but she couldn't be. She had to remember Michael and what he had meant to her. She had to remember that he was the reason why she had come to the Melonga Islands and why she was diving at all.

"Are you coming to Miss Corrigan's party?" she asked him shyly, to change the subject.

"I gather we're to be invaded by Americans, so I think not," he said dryly. "They'll turn the whole thing into a fake Hawaiian Hollywood musical!"

Helen giggled. "Peter calls them the 'blue rinse tourists'," she told him. "I don't think he's expecting anyone younger than retiring age! But I don't see Miss Corrigan allowing anyone to ruin her party, do you?"

He laughed. "No, I don't," he admitted. "What does Peter plan to do with all these people when they do come?"

Helen stood up, stretching her stiff muscles. "He doesn't know!" she chuckled. "He's at his wits' end now. Goodness knows what it will be like when they actually arrive!"

Gregory grunted. "At least I shan't have to be around to see," he said. "You can take me out on the *Sweet Promise* tomorrow. It will give me a chance to see how my leg's behaving." He gave her shoulder a mild pat. "Don't look so horrified," he added, "I'm not planning to dive, but I'll go mad cooped up here much longer!"

It gave her a nice warm feeling that at least they had that in common, but she wouldn't let herself respond to his friendliness. More and more recently she had had to cling to the memory of Michael, and she felt she would be a traitor if she forgot him now. When they were out at sea, she promised herself, she would ask him about Michael and why he had died, and then she could bury his memory for ever. Perhaps, she thought, she would ask him tomorrow.

"I'll see you in the morning, at the jetty?" she said uncertainly.

"Nothing will keep me away!" he said.

She smiled just as the door burst open and Anita came in, a disapproving look on her face. "You'll have to leave, Helen," she said in an important voice. "Can't you see you're tiring him?"

The world was still and strangely silent when Helen stood on the jetty the next morning, waiting for Gregory. No bird sang. Even the sea had gathered itself into a brooding silence and the friendly sound of the light waves lapping against coral sand was noticeable by its absence. The bamboo jetty creaked as Helen walked along it and she was peculiarly aware that it was only the surrounding silence that made her so aware of it. The *Sweet Promise* looked strange too and not quite real. She was badly in need of a coat of paint, Helen noticed, but bathed in early morning light, she looked romantic and lovely. Her furled sails were deep red, wet as they were from dew, and her white-painted sides looked pearly pink as they reflected the rising sun.

Gregory arrived on a pair of crutches that Na-Tinn had made for him. Anita had carefully cushioned the parts that fitted under his arms with foam rubber, and he was already pretty adept at using them.

"I expected you to be on board," he said to Helen.

She stood there, awkwardly, wondering how best to help him. "Can you manage?" she asked at last.

Gregory looked over his shoulder. "Anita is coming to help me," he told her. "She wants to see what the *Sweet Promise* is like anyway. Hadn't you better get on board and see that everything is shipshape?"

Helen felt decidedly unwanted as she jumped on to the narrow deck that was still wet and slippery from the dew, and went forward to check that she had enough cylinders of compressed air and everything else that she would need. The number of cylinders was dangerously low, she thought, but the new supplies had not yet come. She would not be able to stay down for very long on what she had, but perhaps it was just as well, for she hated the thought of leaving Anita too long alone with Gregory. She told herself that her sister-in-law would soon be bored with nothing particular to do, but it wasn't quite that that made her reluctant to be gone for long. She just didn't like much the thought of the two of them being alone together.

When she came back to the cabin, both Gregory and Anita had come on board. She could hear their voices long before she went down the companionway, arguing as to whether it was too early for Anita to make them all some tea. The stillness all about them was unnatural and set Helen's nerves on edge. It was as if the whole of nature was waiting, but waiting for what? She tried to dismiss the matter from her mind, but she still felt taut and uneasy as she hurried down the steps to see how Gregory had stood the business of getting on board.

"I think tea would be a good idea," she said when she saw him. He looked pale and in pain to her.

"Then you can make it," Anita said tartly.

Helen turned on the Calor gas and lit the burner from the box of matches she saw on the table.

"Have you put in the order for more compressed air?" she asked Anita over her shoulder. "We're getting low. We need some helium too. Did Peter tell you? If we do any deep diving we'll need to mix helium in with the oxygen. I just wish we had a decompression chamber that we could sling over the side for when we come up —"

Anita refused to look at her. "I didn't think there was any hurry," she muttered.

"No hurry!" Helen repeated. "Of course there's a hurry! If that frigate rocks about much more on that shelf, it'll fall off and then we'll never get the gold up. It will be lost for ever!"

Anita shrugged. "Gregory won't be diving for a while yet," she said smugly. "Will you?" she said to him, seeking his confirmation. "Helen can't do anything alone, can she?"

"Does that mean that the order hasn't been put in?" he asked, civilly enough.

"Well, Peter did say he didn't think there was any hurry," Anita defended herself sulkily. "You always pick on me!" she added sourly.

Helen gasped, exasperated beyond measure. "I haven't said anything yet," she warned her. "If I were you, I'd wait until I really get started on you!"

Gregory struggled painfully to his feet. "Leave her

alone, Helen," he said. "You could have put in the order yourself if you're really worried!"

"But that's what you *pay* her for!" Helen insisted.

"Then you can leave it to me to see that I get my money's worth," he retorted. "For heaven's sake, stop bickering, and get on with making the tea!"

Helen did so in a stony silence. She had been going to mention the peculiar stillness of the world up on deck, but now she thought better of it. She wouldn't talk to either of them if she didn't have to! She drank her tea in great gulps, the scalding liquid settling in a great hot ball on her stomach. She haughtily refused to sit down when Gregory invited her to do so, reminding him that *someone* had to go up on deck and take the *Sweet Promise* out of the harbour.

"Are you sure you can manage?" he asked her dryly, so that she couldn't be sure if he was joking or not.

"I've been managing all week!" she reminded him swiftly.

He smiled faintly, wincing at the pain in his leg. "Well, I hope you manage it today," he said. "I want to be back for Miss Corrigan's party tonight, even if you don't!"

Helen forbore to reply. It was a long time since she had felt so angry, or indeed so *humiliated* when she had done nothing to deserve it, or nothing that she could see. She was glad to get back up on deck, even though there was not a breath of wind anywhere to fill the sails. They would have to use the engine all the way, she thought, and Gregory would probably find fault with that as well. It would all be *her* fault, of course! She could see it now even before it happened!

Taine-Mal grinned at her cheerfully. "Ready to go?" he asked her. "It's good to have the Boss back on board!"

"Yes, we're ready to go," Helen agreed grumpily.

The Polynesian looked at her with laughing eyes. "I

can see that the typhoon has already arrived in your heart!" he told her.

Helen grunted. "Meaning what?" she asked him.

He pointed out to the sea. "You see how calm and still it is," he said. "And on the Islands too, there is no wind today. And it is quiet. Too quiet to be ordinary. Did you not notice?"

Helen was immediately concerned. "Yes, I noticed," she said. "But I hadn't realised that it meant anything. Does it really mean a typhoon?"

Taine-Mal shrugged. "Too early to tell," he admitted.

"Perhaps we shouldn't go out today?" Helen suggested uncomfortably.

"Okay to go out now," he answered her. "Today, nothing; tomorrow, maybe nothing; next day, probably something!"

Helen tugged nervously at her fingers. "Then we ought to get the gold up before then," she said. "That ship will never stay on the ledge through a storm, let alone a typhoon!"

Taine-Mal's eyes grew dark and round. "You will tell the Boss," he said flatly.

But Helen shook her head. "Not just now," she said firmly. She managed to refrain from adding that nothing would have induced her to say anything to Gregory just then. Taine-Mal wouldn't understand that anyone might have reservations about passing on information to Gregory at any time, let alone when he had just come back from the jaws of death to go out with them.

"Everyone will know at the party tonight," the Polynesian said nonchalantly. "He'll know!"

"If he comes up on deck, he'll be able to see for himself!" Helen added with a confidence she was far from feeling.

"He'll come," he said. "He'll come when he's ready."

Helen started up the engines and watched for her moment to slip the engine into gear as Na-Tinn cast off the ropes fore and aft. They slipped out of the harbour as easily as if Gregory himself had been at the controls. Helen grinned to herself, wishing that he could have been up on deck to see for himself. She had learned quite a lot about the *Sweet Promise* while he had been incapacitated. And she would learn more! She wanted to be a part of the ship as he was, to feel the water beneath her feet and the wind in her hair, to hear the slapping of the sails in the wind and to smell the salty tar smell of the ropes. Only in this weather they wouldn't be able to haul up the sails at all. There wasn't a breath of air to carry them.

Helen didn't hear Gregory come up on deck. She was lost in a world of her own, full of dreams that she couldn't for the life of her have described to anyone. So the shock of his sudden presence was all the greater, making the backs of her hands tingle and doing funny things to her breathing.

"You startled me," she said.

"So I did!" he agreed. "You must have been a long way off not to hear me coming! It wasn't exactly a silent approach."

"No, but I was thinking," she said.

He watched her handling the wheel in silence for a long moment, then he said : "I came up to find out why you weren't using the sails."

"There isn't any air to carry us," she told him.

He looked about him, a slightly startled expression on his face. "I wasn't paying attention," he admitted. "It looks nasty. It's going to make a fine mess of our chances, isn't it?"

She was concerned that he should look so worried. "Taine-Mal says nothing will happen today or tomorrow," she said.

"It will mean my going down with you," he said slowly.

Helen looked as appalled as she felt. "You can't!" she said flatly.

"I can try," he retorted.

He made as if to go back below, dragging his stiff and still painful leg behind him.

"Where are you going?" she demanded.

"I don't see it as any of your business, but I'm going to get ready," he told her.

She stood at the wheel, her eyes blinded with tears, wondering what she could do to prevent him. It was no use pleading, she thought. One might as well plead with a stone! She turned to face him, licking her lips to give her courage. The *Sweet Promise* faltered in her course, but Helen didn't care. Gregory put a strong hand on the wheel and brought her back sharply.

"Why don't you look where you're going?" he asked her gruffly.

Helen abandoned the wheel altogether. "Isn't one death enough?" she said through stiff lips. "Is the gold really worth so much?"

His face looked stony and unyielding. "It wasn't gold that brought about your husband's death, Mrs. Hastings," he said at last. "It was crass carelessness."

Helen drew herself up stiffly. "Oh yes," she said, "I've been meaning to ask you about that—"

"The subject is closed!" he retorted sharply.

"Why?" she insisted sharply. "Because you wrote a letter to his mother explaining how it happened? A letter that I didn't even see?"

"I wrote it to Michael's wife. Why didn't you see it?"

"My mother-in-law is Mrs. Hastings," she sighed. "Naturally the letter came to her hand. Michael belonged to her, after all, so why should I have been interested?" she concluded bitterly.

"So that's why you came?" he said more to himself than to her.

"More or less," she muttered.

He looked at her, and she wished more than ever

that she could tell what he was thinking, but there was no clue to be found in his expression.

"Did you love him so much?" he asked at last.

She shrugged her shoulders. She was beginning to think that she had never loved him at all! "I don't know," she said. "I don't know what I felt about him!"

She was surprised to notice that Gregory was grinning. "Interesting!" he grunted.

"Oh, very!" she retorted, angry because on top of everything else she thought she was going to cry. "Well, do you mean to tell me?"

"Tell you what?" he asked innocently.

Helen stamped her foot with sheer rage. "What happened to him?" she said.

"If you really want to know. He went down when I had told him to wait for me. The frigate was more firmly on the shelf then, but rolling badly in the currents. Michael had cut some kind of an opening on the other side from where we are working now. He managed to pull himself inside. The frigate got caught up in the backlash of some storm, which was why I had told him not to go down alone. She rolled over, cutting off the exit. When we finally got to him it was too late. As it was, we had to rock the frigate dangerously on her perch. She very nearly fell off the shelf altogether. Another storm and she probably will! Satisfied?"

Helen felt devastated. She would not allow herself to dwell on how Michael must have felt as they were trying to get him out. It had been his own fault that he had died, but he had probably never admitted that, even to himself. She wished she could mourn him properly, as a true wife should, but she had no tears left. She had a fleeting vision of his laughing face, and shuddered inwardly at the weakness that his charm had hidden from her for so long. Then his face was gone from her again and, try as she would, she could not recall his features with any clarity at all. He had gone from her for ever.

"He thought he was a better diver than people gave him credit for," she said faintly.

"I'd say he thought he was a better man than he proved to be," Gregory added. "Optimism is a poor stand-in for character."

"That's a cruel thing to say!" she objected quietly.

"It's the truth," he said firmly.

She nodded, turning her back on him as she grasped the wheel again and made a pretence of looking down at the navigational aids to see where they were going.

"The truth can hurt," she said finally.

"Would you rather live with a lie?" he retorted sharply.

"But he's dead. I was his wife. If you knew his mother—" The words jumbled up in her mind. If only he wouldn't look at her like that, almost as if he were waiting for an apology from her. "I must have loved him!" she ended bleakly.

He was silent. He leaned against the rails of the deck, watching her. She would never know what he was really thinking!

"I suppose you think a man should make his own way, no matter what his mother is!" she snapped at him.

"Anita seems able to," he pointed out quietly.

"Perhaps," Helen said without commitment. "Perhaps she hasn't been tested yet."

"Perhaps not, but she has enough love in her to meet most challenges. She has a strength that her brother lacked."

Had Michael lacked love? Helen didn't know. She would never know now, she thought. They had been married for such a short time, and in some ways she had never known him at all.

"I tried to love him," she said.

Gregory looked at her for a long moment. "He was luckier than he knew," he said so gently that she was surprised. "And very much luckier than he deserved!" he added thoughtfully.

Helen hugged the compliment to her. "Oh, do you think so?" she gasped, blushing faintly at the rush of feeling within her.

He reached forward and brushed a lock of hair that had escaped from her eyes. "I'd better get back down below," he told her. "Anita will be wondering what's happened to me. Can you manage up here?"

She grasped the wheel firmly with both hands, wondering at her disappointment at his going. "I've managed before!" she said dryly.

He grinned. "Good," he said. "I knew I could rely on you!"

She felt lonely when he had gone, but then she had to get used to that. It was the lot of widows to feel lonely, she told herself harshly, and who was she to quarrel with that?

# CHAPTER NINE

BY midday Gregory was sniffing the weather as often as the two Polynesian sailors. "It's coming," he remarked. "But not today!"

Anita laughed. She was rather looking forward to a full-scale storm. She had read about typhoons, but she had experienced nothing more serious than the downpour after a thunderstorm. A typhoon didn't seem quite real; it sounded more romantic and exotic than dangerous.

"How about tomorrow?" Helen asked. She was checking their equipment after she had made her first dive and she was depressed by the thought of the little compressed air they had going spare.

"Tomorrow okay!" Na-Tinn told her.

Helen glanced at Gregory through her eyelashes. Did he believe that too?

"Who cares about tomorrow?" Anita said comfortably. "Miss Corrigan's party will be over by then. It would be a shame if it were to spoil that!"

But at that moment Helen was more concerned with her own problems. "I hope we have enough compressed air to last out," she said, still worried. "What about tomorrow?"

Na-Tinn smelt the air, opening his nostrils wide, his eyes half-closed in concentration. "No typhoon tomorrow morning," he promised her. "Afternoon?" He shrugged his shoulders. "Wouldn't like to say," he said.

Helen's eyes met Gregory's. "That doesn't give us very long, does it?" she said anxiously.

"If you can manage today, I'll go down with you tomorrow morning and we'll bring up the gold," Gregory said.

"But you can't!" she protested.

"I can try!" he retorted.

She leaned back, smiling at him. "And who said that optimism was no substitute for character?" she teased him gently.

His laughter mingled with hers. "You mind your business and I'll mind mine," he offered. "How big a hole have you knocked into the side of the frigate?"

"More than big enough for us to get in and out," she told him. She shivered suddenly, despite the hot sun. "It looks black inside and rather horrid. I'm not much looking forward to it."

"Do you think you can get everything rigged up for us today?" he asked her. "We'll have to make a quick trip in the morning if we're going to get away with it."

"I think so," she agreed. "I'll have to rig up some kind of lighting. Perhaps we could leave the lines rigged up to a marker buoy and hope that nothing interferes with them overnight."

He nodded. "I'll help all I can from up here," he said briskly. "You'd better get ready for the next dive."

It took a long time to fix up all the necessary wires and to make sure that the powerful bulbs were working. When she switched them on, several curious fish came to see what she was doing. They showed no fear at swimming in and out of the gaping hole she had made in the side of the frigate. She was tempted to put her head through the gap and see what she could see with the help of the lights, but she was very conscious of how little compressed air they had left. There was not enough for her to waste any of it, and she still had such a great deal to do. Gregory had a plan of the frigate in the saloon of the *Sweet Promise*, but they had got no idea from it as to where the gold had been stored. Helen favoured the captain's cabin as the most likely place, but to get there they would have to go right through the sunken ship. When she had turned over, she had made things a great deal more awkward for them all.

When at last she had done, she saw by her gauge that she had only a few seconds in which to surface before her cylinders of air were completely empty. She was cross with herself for cutting it so fine. She liked to come up slowly, without any strain, for she had long ago discovered that most of the bad effects that could follow a dive, like headaches and a feeling of nausea, depended on how one came up. To come up too quickly was never a good idea.

But there was nothing she could do this time but to surface as quickly as she could. She took in a final deep breath of compressed air and felt herself bobbing upwards like a cork. There was a rushing sensation in her ears and she felt dizzy, but then there was the warm sun on her face and she tore off her mask, spitting out the mouthpiece, and took in some great gulps of air.

It was Gregory who helped her back on board. "Why didn't you come up before?" he asked her angrily. "What did you think you were doing?"

"He's been as cross as two sticks!" Anita added sourly.

Helen forced a smile. "It's all ready for tomorrow," she gasped.

"Why didn't you take two trips over it?" Gregory demanded, still angry.

"I keep telling you, we're running short of compressed air," she murmured. "I didn't want to waste any."

Anita clapped a hand over her mouth. "Don't start him off again on that," she pleaded. "I've had nothing else ever since you went down. I don't think coming out here agrees with him. He's been like a bear with a sore head all afternoon!"

Helen smiled despite herself. She felt a great deal

better. If he knew how low their stocks were, then she needn't worry any longer, she thought comfortably. It was pleasant and warm on the deck and she shut her eyes to turn her face to the sun. She must indeed have been tired, for in a few seconds she was fast asleep.

When Helen awoke, someone had carried her down below and had deposited her on to one of the berths in the forecabin. She wriggled her legs and felt the rough warmth of the blanket that had been flung over her. She sat up quickly and looked out of the porthole. The sun had just set and the last light was falling away below the horizon. In another few minutes it would be completely dark. How on earth long had she been asleep? She glanced at her watch, but she hadn't got it on. It didn't really matter, she decided, for the engines were still going so they couldn't have arrived back in harbour. And the sleep had done her good. She felt as fresh now as she had when she had started !

A soft knock at the door preceded Anita bringing her a cup of tea.

"Gregory said to wake you," she said. "I do think you might have got up earlier, though, Helen. He's had to do everything to get us back to harbour !"

"I can't think why I fell asleep," Helen apologised. "I don't usually !"

Anita sniffed. "Gregory seems to think you've been doing too much recently," she informed her coldly.

"Has he been beastly?" Helen asked sympathetically.

Anita looked shocked. "I don't think Gregory is ever beastly," she said daintily. "He's a bit worried, that's all. Not that he need have been, as I told him. His leg is quite enough for him to worry about !"

"Well, I think he can be beastly!" Helen said thoughtfully. "In fact he can be nastier than anyone else I know!"

Anita smiled a superior smile. "I thought you reserved that for my mother," she reminded her. "And with a great deal more justification!" she added justly.

Helen sipped at her tea and swung her legs on to the floor, stretching herself as she prepared to get up. "Don't remind me!" she exclaimed. "I'd forgotten for the moment!"

"Then you don't think so badly of Gregory, do you?" Anita went on smugly. "You can't really think he's nasty!"

Helen wondered briefly why her sister-in-law should be so concerned with what she thought about anybody. She frowned thoughtfully. "He can be quite nice too—sometimes," she said judiciously.

Anita giggled. "I think you like him more than you're saying!" she observed. "And it's no good getting cross! I know how you used to look at Michael sometimes! You'd go all dreamy and thoughtful about him."

More annoyed than she could say, Helen struggled into her clothes. "And what has that to do with it?" she demanded darkly.

Her sister-in-law blinked. "N—nothing," she said nervously. "Only, Helen, don't you think that Gregory sometimes has that effect too?"

"On every female within a radius of fifty miles!" Helen agreed crossly.

Anita sighed. "I suppose so," she admitted. "But I wish it were Peter. He's more like Michael, don't you think?"

Helen hadn't thought about it at all, but she was prepared to agree to anything so that they could talk about something else besides Gregory de Vaux. She grew muddled whenever she thought of him, and she preferred to have all her thoughts neat and logical—and manageable!

"Do you like Peter?" she asked Anita with interest.

To her surprise, her sister-in-law took a long time to answer. "I hardly know," she said at last. "He has a terrific admiration for you, Helen. At least, he hopes to dance with you tonight. He told me so!"

"With me?" Helen repeated. It would be nice and comfortable to have Peter Harmon as her escort to Miss Corrigan's party, she thought happily. "Good!" she said out loud. "I hope he does dance with me!" And she wondered why Anita gave her such an odd look before she took her empty cup back to the saloon.

The whole hotel had been decorated for Miss Corrigan's party. Palm leaves hung from the ceilings in clusters, the water in the swimming pool had been coloured a delicious deep shade of green, and there were coconuts, carefully prepared, for all the guests to drink from. It was strange at first to see the empty hotel come to life under the presence of its American guests. They were everywhere, determined to make the most of their short stay in the Islands. The novelty of everything appealed to them, and that they should be included so readily in Miss Corrigan's party went straight to their hearts. They were unanimous in their determination that the party should really swing!

Miss Corrigan herself was all that was gracious. She fell easily into the part, despite her large, bulky figure and the uncompromising style in which she wore her hair.

"There must be plenty of everything," she had told Peter. "I won't have anything skimped. Tell the boys to get busy bringing in the lobsters, clams, and everything else, will you?"

Peter had been rather nonplussed at first. He was accustomed to importing all his needs from the States, and he was frankly astonished at how this elderly spinster set about things. He had not known that the Islands could produce such a variety of foods. For, apart from all the seafoods, there were sweet potatoes, pineapples and other fruits, sucking-pigs all ready to be baked in the traditional manner, sweet corn, piled up cob upon cob, and so many coconuts that he gave up trying to count them. It seemed the whole Melongese people had combined to provide Miss Corrigan with everything that she might need, most of them refusing to accept anything at all by way of payment.

The whole day had been spent in these lavish preparations. Peter had been everywhere at once, working harder than he had since he had been chosen to manage the hotel.

"I missed you," he said to Anita. "I've got used to having you around!"

Anita looked pleased. "I wish I had been here—in a way," she said shyly. "It was nice being on the boat, of course, but I wondered what you were doing here—"

"Were they kind to you?" he shot at her.

"Of course they were!" she insisted. "There was a bit of an upset because the supplies hadn't come, but they seemed to get over that."

Peter groaned. "Oh lord! I forgot to tell you. I told them to leave their stuff off for this trip. I thought we'd need such a lot of stuff for this party and I didn't think there'd be any hurry—"

Anita giggled nervously. "I don't think it matters," she soothed him, then she wrinkled up her brow thoughtfully. "Quite honestly, I think they take everything far too seriously. There wasn't a breath of wind today, but they did nothing but talk about some typhoon or other, just as if it were going to come upon us at any moment. It would be quite exciting, wouldn't it?"

Peter grinned. "I'll believe it when I see it!" he agreed.

Helen stood awkwardly in the centre of the foyer, knowing that she shouldn't be listening to someone else's conversation.

"It's easy to see that neither of you have ever been in a typhoon!" she said loudly, to remind them that she was there.

"Have you?" Anita enquired sweetly.

Helen shook her head. "But I've heard my father speaking about them," she said.

Anita smiled gently. "That hardly makes you an expert, darling," she drawled. "I expect Peter knows far more about it than you do."

Helen had no such faith. "We ought to go and change," she suggested, hoping to change the subject. "Almost everybody else has come downstairs. Doesn't it all look *pretty*?"

Anita looked about her, wide-eyed and suddenly gay. "Oh, it does!" she agreed. "I've never seen anything so pretty. You've done a marvellous job, Peter!"

Helen was conscious of Peter's eyes on her face, expecting her to join in the praise, but somehow the words stuck in her throat. She knew that Peter hadn't really been responsible for them, that had been Miss Corrigan and, although there was no reason for her not to congratulate him as well as the old lady, she couldn't bring herself to do so.

"Come on," she said urgently to Anita. "We must go and change!"

The lifts were occupied, so they raced each other up the stairs, clattering up them as fast as they could go. When they arrived on the floor where they were now sleeping, they were breathless and unable to speak.

"I'm glad I kept my prettiest dress for tonight," Anita said when she could. "What are you going to wear?"

Helen smiled softly. "Lace over a shocking pink petticoat," she said. "It's by far the nicest dress I have."

Anita hesitated. "But do you think you ought to?" she asked frankly.

"Why not?"

Anita coloured. "Well, you being a widow," she said awkwardly. "It isn't the same, is it?"

Helen was frankly surprised. "What do you expect me to wear?" she demanded. "Black crepe?"

"Of course not!" Anita muttered. "Only *shocking pink*, Helen? Michael wouldn't have liked it, would he?"

"Michael won't be here to see me!" Helen snapped. She went into her room and slammed the door shut behind her. Would Michael have objected? She couldn't be sure. But she could be sure that she didn't care! It wasn't *Michael* that she wanted to please tonight! She was going to please herself! She told herself that often while she was dressing, but she knew even then that it was only a half-truth. The one she really wanted to please was unlikely to notice, but in case he did— In case he did, she took a great deal of care with her hair and even more care with her make-up. She thought she looked quite pretty when she had finished at her dressing-table and stood in the centre of the room, looking at herself in the long glass, as she swept first the shocking pink watered silk petticoat over her head and then the hand-made lace dress. When she had done, even she was astonished by the result. She felt a little prick of pleasure in the back of her spine as she knew herself to be looking truly beautiful. He couldn't help but notice, she thought with pride, she looked like a new person; a younger, gayer version of her old self, a young girl ready for love.

Anita was still disapproving when they met at the lift

shaft. "Honestly, Helen, I think you look lovely," she said, "but it isn't *right*! It'll give everybody the wrong idea!"

"And who is everybody?" Helen asked, her voice catching ominously in the back of her throat.

"Well," Anita said unhappily, "Mr. de Vaux for one! I'm sure he's very susceptible——"

"*Gregory*!" Helen could feel the tingling sensation in her spine again. "Do you really think Gregory will notice?" she asked with interest, unable to conceal her pleasure at the idea.

"He could hardly help it!" Anita snorted. "But at least he can look after himself. What about Peter?"

Helen had to bite the inside of her lower lip to keep herself from laughing. "Oh yes, Peter," she agreed carefully. "Peter won't care!"

"I don't see how you can be so sure!" Anita complained. "He was asking about you all over again. I told him you were still getting over Michael and weren't interested in anyone else, but he's hardly going to believe me with you in that dress!"

Helen shook her skirts and listened with satisfaction to the rustle they made. "You're looking lovely in your dress too!" she told Anita firmly. "I've never seen you looking half so pretty!"

Anita preened herself happily. "Do you really think so! Oh, Helen, you are good to me, bringing me here and everything!"

Helen kissed her gently on the cheek. "Have a lovely evening," she told her. "And try not to worry about me! I'll behave very well, I promise you!"

Anita bit her lip and looked away from her. "As well as they'll allow you to!" she said sharply. "Peter promised the first dance to me, but——"

Helen's eyes widened slowly as she looked at her sister-in-law. "I don't think I shall be dancing much with Peter," she said immediately. "To tell the truth, it's one thing to get all dressed up, but another to dance all night. I don't think I want to dance much at all!"

Anita's relief was so patent that Helen nearly laughed. But she was more than a little cross too, for she loved to dance and had been looking forward to it all day. Oh well, she thought, she'd join Miss Corrigan on the sidelines and watch the others as a widow should. It was another thing about widowhood that she would have to learn—if she could!

Miss Corrigan, however, had no intention of sitting on any sidelines. She had taken the Hawaiian-type band aside and had drilled them carefully in their duties. "As many Island dances as possible!" she had roared at them. "If no one else can do them, I can! It will loosen them all up to swing their hips! Have you heard me?"

They all laughed like mad. "Sure thing!" they shouted back in unison.

The guests were cautious at first, but most of them managed something that resembled the graceful Island dances and they were all eager to learn how to do it properly.

"You show them, Helen," Miss Corrigan said at last, exhausted by her own efforts. "And slow the music down! Do it by yourself, girl! Show them how it should be done!"

Helen was shy at first, but the music caught at her and she could no more have stood still than died. She made a nervous start, not sure that she could remember the steps that her father had taught her so long before, but after the first few seconds the rhythm was enough and she didn't have to think at all. She shut her eyes and gave herself up to the music. It was the loveliest feeling, to sway as gently as a palm-tree in the wind and then to break out as the music quickened, into a dance that spoke easily of her loneliness and her sadness and the curious fancies that haunted her dreams.

When the music came to an end, it was the Islanders who led the applause. Helen opened her eyes, embarrassed by the mild sensation she had caused. "I—I learned as a child," she explained baldly, and did her best to lose herself in the crowd of dancers that edged the space that had been cleared for her solo performance.

"I thought you said you weren't going to dance!" Anita accosted her fiercely.

"I shouldn't have done!" Helen admitted. "I'd forgotten—"

"And in that dress!" Anita added in a shocked voice.

"What's wrong with the dress?" a masculine voice demanded, and Helen was horrified to discover that she had run practically straight into Gregory's arms.

"It isn't really suitable for a widow," Helen told him breathlessly. "Only it's pretty and I wanted—"

Gregory's enigmatic eyes looked the dress over carefully. "Very revealing," he said with laughter running through his voice, "but not half as revealing as that dance!"

Helen drew herself up. "I wouldn't have called it particularly revealing!" she said witheringly. "It has rather a modest neckline, in my opinion!"

"Oh, quite!" he agreed.

"Michael wouldn't have liked it," Anita put in nervously.

"Well, that's a point in its favour!" Gregory drawled.

"It may be in your opinion," Helen informed him loftily, "but to me it matters a great deal what Michael would have thought—"

"Rubbish!" Gregory said roundly.

Helen stared at him. "How can you—"

Gregory cut her off with an impatient gesture. "You don't give a damn for what Michael would have thought! Even supposing that he thought about you at all!" He forced her chin up so that her eyes met his. "You're less of a hypocrite when you don't bother to think, Helen Hastings," he told her roughly. "You'd better get back on the dancing floor."

"But I don't want to dance any more," she said breathlessly.

He laughed unkindly. "If you think I can't dance because of my leg, you're very much mistaken!" he almost shouted at her. "And you'll dance with me! And you'll like it!"

There didn't seem to be any future in arguing with him. Already she thought a lot of people must be looking at them, and the very last thing she wanted was to go on being in the centre of attention.

"All right," she said. "I'll dance with you—and if you open up your leg it will be *your* fault!"

He grinned, but he said nothing. His arm went round her and held her tightly against him. It was the first time she had ever been so close to him, except when he had handed over the wheel to her on the *Sweet Promise*, and she didn't remember that it had been at all like this!

"If you would allow me to breathe—" she said aloud. "Or am I holding you up, as well as dancing with you?"

"That tongue of yours will get you into trouble one of these days," he warned her. "Is that better?"

It wasn't better at all! Even with him standing away from her as if they were strangers and didn't approve of each other at all, she still had difficulty in breathing properly, a sensation which she didn't like and didn't intend to put up with.

"This is ridiculous!" she said sharply. "Have you forgotten that you're supposed to be diving in the morning?"

"Helen, can't you relax and shut up?" he pleaded with her.

"But I'm worried—"

"Then don't !" he advised. He broke away from her, looking down at her with exasperation. "If I hadn't seen you with my own eyes—" he began.

"Seen me what?" she asked him nervously.

*"Dance!"* He waved to the band and they broke out into another Island number, grinning and nudging at one another as they did so.

"But we can't dance this !" Helen protested feebly, for already the music had set her feet following the rhythm whether she would or no.

"Why not?" he asked, his arm coming round her again as tightly as before.

"It's a courting dance," she murmured. "It isn't proper !"

His laugh caught in the back of his throat. "My lovely Helen, you have the oddest ideas of propriety," he said. "I should have said it was eminently suitable !"

But Helen wasn't even listening. In the music she could hear all sorts of things that she had forgotten about for more years than she could remember. In it was the sound of love and growing things, and the spinning world reached out for the destiny that awaited it. In it were her own beginnings and the beginnings of the man who stood beside her and who danced it with her. It was a dangerous, persuasive sound that promised who knew what?

The band thudded out the rhythm with the hollow sound of a bare hand on dug-out wooden drums. A guitar or two, of local manufacture, added the sweeter sound of the melody, while a flute and a home-made whistle sounded the counterpoint that completed the complicated pattern of sound. When they saw that Helen and Gregory could interpret the music and follow it as they would themselves in their own dances, they settled down to the sheer joy of playing, complicating the beat and adding words that no one but themselves could understand in a compulsive, husky undertone. One by one, the other dancers fell out, content merely to sway in time to the music, and to watch someone else who could turn the dance into a living, breathing thing before their eyes.

She should never have allowed it, Helen thought desperately. She knew the ending would have to come. The drums hurried out a quicker and quicker beat, and the singing became louder, burning her ears although she had no idea of their meaning. Then, in the middle of a phase, the music stopped. There was a long moment of silence, and then a crashing crescendo of sound that drew her closer to Gregory. She was almost expecting it when his lips came down on hers and she was kissed more soundly than she had ever been.

"Oh, how could you?" she asked him miserably.

"Very easily!" he assured her.

"That's what I thought," she said bitterly. "That's what a dress and Island music will do for you! You can't pretend that it means a thing! Anita was quite right—"

"Helen—"

She put her hands over her ears. "I won't listen! I won't! I won't! And I won't dance with you again! Not ever!"

He allowed her to leave the floor and she should have been pleased that he didn't follow her, but she wasn't. She saw Anita dancing with Peter and tried to smile at her, but found she couldn't. Her whole face felt frozen and odd. She wanted to leave the party then and there, but she knew that Miss Corrigan would be hurt if she did. There was nothing to prevent her going upstairs for a moment or two, though, where she could calm herself, and tell herself what a fool she was.

When she came downstairs again, she had resigned herself to a sober future that consisted largely of hard work and well-schooled emotions kept severely in the background where they belonged. That such a future gave her very little pleasure even to think about was something she was determined to keep entirely to herself. After all, there was more to life than floating round a ballroom, or dancing primitive dances in a spectacular and unsuitable dress. But was there, an unbidden voice inside her demanded, more to life than the subtle chemistry that passed between a man and a woman at any time? But that was another thing that, at that moment, she was in no mood to admit.

# CHAPTER TEN

MISS CORRIGAN thought with satisfaction that it was the best party she had ever given. The music had been good, the food was better, and the American guests, with their customary generosity, had done everything they could to enjoy themselves. It had been an exhausting evening. There had been so much to do. Miss Corrigan had felt obliged to personally oversee the roasting of the sucking pigs, helping to make the clay ovens and even to wrap the pigs in the leaves that gave that special delicate flavour. Then she had had to choose the lobsters and see that they were properly dressed. And there had been the clams to bake and the Island people to entertain, because she wouldn't have had them feel left out for worlds. But it had all ended very satisfactorily and she felt she could relax now and enjoy herself by joining in with the dancing outside.

Miss Corrigan had lived for so long on the Islands that she felt more at home there than with the more civilised West. She was enchanted by the fairy lights that hung everywhere and the seductive music that she knew from experience would go on all night, only to die away with the first rays of the dawning sun.

When she caught a glimpse of Helen's dress, she thought at first that she was still with Gregory and was pleased, but then she saw that the girl was alone, leaning against a palm-tree, listening to the Island music as it went on all about her.

"I thought you were dancing!" she said roughly to the girl, noting her startled expression as she was brought back to reality with a bump. "Does something to you, this music, doesn't it?"

148

"I prefer it out here," Helen answered.

Miss Corrigan nodded briskly. "Even the Islanders are growing sophisticated," she said. "A few years ago and they would have died at the thought of playing for outsiders."

Helen smiled. "Out here they are playing for themselves," she observed. "I thought at first it was the same as Hawaiian music, but it isn't, is it?"

"All Polynesian music is much the same," Miss Corrigan told her. "From the Maoris to the Melongese, you get the same beautiful melodies. The same grass skirts too, some people will tell you, but I find them very different from island to island, even in this little group."

"You love them, don't you?" Helen said.

"I wouldn't have stayed here so long if I didn't!" Miss Corrigan said frankly. "How about you?"

"Me?" Helen sounded startled. She didn't want to talk about herself. "I shan't be here for very much longer," she said. "Tomorrow we'll bring up the gold with any luck and then there'll be nothing for me to stay for."

Miss Corrigan looked sad. "I rather hoped you might find something to stay for," she suggested.

But Helen shook her head positively. "There's nothing for me here. Nothing at all! It's been a pleasant interlude, but now I have to get on with my life. I want to find something to do that's worthwhile and—and *suitable*."

"Suitable?" Miss Corrigan repeated with raised eyebrows. "My dear girl, are you sure you know what you're talking about?"

Helen was silent. She was still smarting inwardly from her dance with Gregory and she wasn't prepared to talk about it. "I must go to bed," she said instead. "I want to be fresh for the morning. It's going to be quite a day!"

"Very well," Miss Corrigan agreed easily. "I'll say goodnight to you, then."

"Goodnight," Helen responded. "It was a lovely party, Miss Corrigan. Thank you very much."

"The party was for my own pleasure," Miss Corrigan retorted sharply. "Helen, look after Gregory tomorrow, won't you?"

Helen stiffened. "I'll do my best, but he's more than capable of looking after himself. He won't thank me if I interfere!"

"Is it thanks you're looking for?" Miss Corrigan asked her innocently.

Helen refused to answer. She watched Miss Corrigan disappear through the palm trees and be greeted by her Islanders. She was totally at home amongst them, they were like her own family, so how could she know how Helen felt, who had no family and no place of her own?

There was no one about whom she knew when she made her way inside to the lift. There was a lot of laughter and a few people were still dancing, but with midnight the party was coming to an end. Helen stepped into the lift and pressed the button that would take her up to her floor. It hardly took a moment to remove her finery and to wash the make-up from her face. She slipped into a nightgown and pushed back the bedclothes ready to get into bed. She was very, very tired and it was important for her to get to sleep, but sleep had never seemed further away. It seemed to her that whenever she shut her eyes she could hear Anita saying coldly, "Michael would not have approved!"

When she slept, it was to dream of her mother-in-law. There were flashes of happiness that came to nothing as the elder Mrs. Hastings took the moments away from her, one by one. When Helen half-stirred and woke, she dismissed her firmly from her mind, but there was still Michael to point an accusing finger at her whenever Gregory's shadow crossed her path. She was Michael's widow, *Michael's widow*! She was lost before she began.

In the cold light of dawn she felt drawn and exhausted. She didn't have to go to the window to see if the uncanny stillness was still with them, she could feel it all about her where she lay.

Gregory walked along the jetty with only a stick to help him. He limped rather, but otherwise he looked much as usual, his bare feet slapping against the bamboo.

"No Anita today?" he called out to Helen.

"She's helping Peter to clear up after the party," she told him. She wondered if she should offer to help him on board, but there was something in his eyes that forbade her.

"Have you checked the equipment?" he asked her curtly.

She made a face. She had checked it at least half a dozen times and it still meant that they were cutting things finer than they should. If it had not been for the coming typhoon, nothing would have induced her to go out today before their fresh supplies had arrived.

"We'll make it—if we're lucky!" she said awkwardly.

His disapproval was clear to see. "Luck shouldn't come into it. However, I suppose it can't be helped. Na-Tinn! Taine-Mal! Jump to it! I want to leave straight away!"

Helen went below as soon as she could. Quite suddenly she felt better and able to laugh at herself. She rejoiced that she was dressed once more in grubby jeans and an American shirt, it was just as though her troubles had gone with the elaborate dress of the night before. It hadn't been *her* that he had kissed at all! It had been a pretty stranger in a very pretty dress who had been banished from his thoughts as easily as the music that had inspired their dance together. She had been ridiculous to worry! If he could dismiss the incident so easily, why so could she!

She was humming as she made herself some coffee, scraping out the instant grounds from the bottom of the tin. She couldn't put a name to the tune, but it was pretty and she liked it.

"Is any of that coffee for me?" Gregory asked her, coming into the saloon as the *Sweet Promise* slipped from the harbour.

"It will be rather weak," she apologised.

"Are we running out of coffee too?" he said irritably.

"It looks like it," she answered cheerfully.

He drank his coffee in silence. He drank it black, without any sugar, because otherwise he felt it would be so weak that he wouldn't be able to taste it at all.

"Anita will have to go!" he said at last.

"What?" she said. Whatever she had expected him to say, it hadn't been that!

"She'll have to go," he repeated. "She's unreliable. When we move on from here, we can't continue to carry her."

Helen stared at him in silence.

"Don't look so surprised!" he went on irritably. "You know as well as I do that she's done practically nothing for her pay!"

"That isn't fair!" Helen protested automatically.

"Oh, isn't it?" he retorted. "Then what would you do about her?"

"I don't think we'll have to bother," Helen heard herself saying. "She seems quite interested in the hotel."

Gregory laughed. "In Peter Harmon, you mean! Well, good luck to her!"

Helen drank her coffee with dignity. She wanted to ask him where he was going when he left the

Islands, and why he should include her, but she didn't like to. She had only just recovered her balance after her run in with him the night before and she wasn't ready to take any risks.

"Are you sure you'll be able to dive?" she asked instead.

"Just as well as I can dance!" he said flatly.

Helen swallowed. "Then you must be feeling pretty fit," she said mildly. "I don't fancy going down alone!" She shivered at the thought, and hoped he hadn't noticed. But he had, of course. His eyes softened and he grinned at her.

"Don't worry!" he said. "I'll be there!"

She might have retorted that it didn't matter to her one way or the other, but she was too honest for that. There were many things that she could do alone, but going into that black hole that she had cut in the side of the frigate was not one of them. For that she needed his presence, *his* presence, for no one else would do for that.

"I think I'll go and get ready," she said.

"Okay," he drawled. "I'll see you on deck."

She didn't go up on deck though until they had sighted the marker buoys she had left above the wreck the day before. They sat there, exactly where she had left, motionless on a motionless sea.

Taine-Mal helped her into the harness which held the cylinders of compressed air and her other equipment, and then she went over the side without waiting for Gregory, wanting to check on her work before he came. She thought she had imagined the faint breeze that seemed to cross the surface of the water, but a second later when she saw the buoys rocking, she knew that the wind was indeed getting up.

"Are you sure the typhoon isn't coming?" she asked the Polynesians.

They shook their heads. "There is time yet," they said in unison.

Helen wasn't entirely convinced. The breeze was rippling the surface of the water now, chasing a thousand tiny waves in patterns over the sea. It was coming, she knew that. There was not a bird to be seen, not even the usual friendly gulls who squawked overhead wherever the *Sweet Promise* went. She watched as Gregory slipped into the water beside her and knew that he was worried too.

"We shall have to hurry," she almost pleaded with him.

He nodded, not wasting the time to talk. "Is everything ready?"

Helen signalled to Na-Tinn to turn on the lights and through the water they could see the frigate light up down below them, revealing the grey shadowy sides and the great hole that had been cut in her side. There were no fish to be seen. They had already taken cover from the great storm that was to come.

Gregory nodded again and struck out for the depths. In the water, one could barely see that he had been injured. He sank as easily as ever, going ahead first for the bottom. Helen adjusted her breathing gear and followed him. It was a peculiar feeling, swimming through the gently stirring waters towards the lit-up wreck, with its barnacled bottom and its nose crushed into the coral shelf that held it.

Gregory looked calm, almost indifferent, through his mask. He pointed towards the hole in the frigate and picked up one of the portable lights she had rigged up for this very moment. He held it out to her, and she took it, swathing the yards of flex over her shoulder so that she could pay it out, foot by foot, as they ventured deep inside the frigate.

The swell in the water was rising rapidly and she

could hear the hull of the wreck grating against the coral shelf. Her heart beat so rapidly that she could feel her pulse against the rubber straps of her face-mask. She was sweating with fear, but her hands didn't tremble, she noticed proudly. She was holding that light as steady as if she had had both feet planted on mother earth! The next moment was going to be the worst one, when she saw Gregory pull himself inside the frigate and she would have to follow him, carrying the light.

The actuality wasn't as bad as she had thought it would be. It was as black as ink inside, with only the single beam from the light to cast strange, grey shadows wherever she looked. But she no longer believed in strange monsters, or squids as big as whales waiting for her in one of the forsaken cabins. Now that the moment was actually upon her, she was quite interested in the ship and the curious, rather sad remnants of her former life that were still intact.

They knew exactly where they were going from the plan of the frigate that Gregory had set out in the saloon of the *Sweet Promise*. In a way it detracted from their exploration of the ghostly insides of the ship, for it was all so exactly as they had thought it would be. They could find their way unerringly from one cabin to another, from ward-room to wardroom, and down to the engines.

The crunching noise of the metal against the coral shelf was muffled by the sides of the ship, but it was loud enough to give them an increasing sense of urgency as they tried to get through to the captain's cabin. The door had fallen shut and it was a hard struggle to pull it open against the weight of the water, but Gregory finally managed it, wedging himself against the roof of the corridor outside.

He held the door open and waved her to go in first. Helen held the light up as high as she could and peered through the gloom into the small space which was the goal of the whole operation. The ship lurched ominously beneath their feet. Oh, hurry, hurry, Helen prayed. If the ship were to be rocked off the shelf now with them inside her, they would never get out alive. They *must hurry*!

Gregory pointed to a small safe that was fastened into the wall of the cabin and Helen's heart sank. They would never get it open, and they would never retrieve the gold. But she reckoned without Gregory's determination. He had picked up from somewhere a bar of solid iron and with this he attacked the safe as if his life depended on it. He managed to get a corner of the bar wedged into a crack between the safe and the wall and with a quite horrid groaning sound, the safe came free and sank into the gloomy waters.

Helen pointed the light downwards, caught a glimpse of the precious safe, and hooked it up with her free hand. Gregory gave her a thumbs-up signal and they shot out of the cabin as fast as they could go, retracing their way back the way they had come.

Helen thought that she would never have such a feeling of relief as she experienced when they saw the hole in the side of the frigate before them. Even as they crawled out on to the coral shelf they could feel the swelling currents around them. Gregory looked round anxiously and saw that the nose of the frigate had already worked free. Without pausing even to make sure that Helen still had the safe in her hand, he threw the light away from her and grabbed her hand, pulling her up to the surface behind him.

Beneath them, the frigate rolled restlessly, rocking against the coral shelf and breaking off large hunks of the pretty, fragile substance, built out of the millions and millions of skeletons left behind by the tiny creatures who had once lived there. Then, almost sucking them down with her, the frigate rose and fell slowly into the bottomless depths below the shelf.

It was a sad ending. Helen hardly noticed when Gregory took the safe from her. Her eyes stung with unshed tears and she could barely see out of her mask. It was only then that she realised that she had surfaced and that she didn't have to hold her breath any longer. She pulled off her mask and spat out the mouthpiece, breathing in the soft, salty air as though she had never breathed fresh air before.

Na-Tinn waved at her excitedly, almost falling off the deck.

"You have it! You have it!" he screamed.

"We have the safe," Gregory shouted to him. "We've yet to find out if the gold is inside!"

But nothing could depress their spirits just then. They dragged the equipment on board with willing hands, leaving it in a dripping, tangled mess of wires, lights, cylinders and collapsed buoys, all over the deck. The wind was quite fresh by now. It was strange how quickly it had come up. It was hard to believe that it was hardly an hour since it had been so still and calm that the sea had looked more like a painting than real. It was real enough now, with the waves, though not yet big, rolling ominously as a warning of what was to come.

Gregory took one look at Helen and sent her down below. "It'll be blowing up quite a storm before we can make harbour," he warned her. "You'd better stay down there and keep warm."

"And you?" Helen asked him, aware that he was limping badly now and that his leg must be paining him badly.

"I'll come as soon as we've got the sails up. We'll have to take a reef in the mainsail, but Na-Tinn can go up aloft. I've had it!"

There was no need to tell the Polynesian sailors that Gregory was tired. They eased him into the cockpit, cracking jokes to each other to cover up their concern for him. "Soon be plenty wind to carry us home," Taine-Mal said gaily. He began to hum the tune that Helen had been singing earlier, a broad grin on his face.

Gregory held on to the wheel until they were well clear of the reef and scuttling through the uncertain wind for home. Then he went below to join Helen.

"Have you got the safe open yet?" he asked her.

"I haven't tried," she answered. "Now, I've heated up some soup. Do you want some?"

"I'd rather have some coffee or tea, but I suppose soup is all we've got?"

Helen chuckled. "I didn't think we had that!" she said.

She set the two mugs on the table and filled them with the boiling liquid in the saucepan. The mugs slid across the table and back again, reminding them of the weather outside.

"Will we get back in time?" Helen asked, trying to keep her voice as steady as her hand.

Gregory's eyes met hers. "I don't know," he admitted frankly. "Even if we do, we'll really feel the swell before we get into harbour. Are you a good sailor, Helen?"

She smiled. "I pride myself on it," she answered.

They laughed together and Helen felt better. The *Sweet Promise* was a strongly made vessel, even if she could do with a fresh coat of paint, and she had confidence that if anyone could sail her through a typhoon, that person would be Gregory de Vaux!

"Shall we get the safe open?" she suggested. "I'd love to see if the gold really is inside!"

"It looks a pretty solid job," Gregory said doubtfully. "We may have to get a safe-cracker on the job. I don't know if bashing it will do much good."

"We can try," she pleaded. "Here, have a go with these knives!"

There were traces of rust on the back of the safe. The tell-tale red stains spread out from a spot in the centre, under the encrusted surface of the metal. In places, a layer or two of the metal had disappeared entirely, but what was left was as solid as ever and would probably have stood up to a pick-axe, let alone their futile attemps with a couple of kitchen knives.

"I'm going to see what's happening," Gregory said. "I think I'll drop the sails and carry on with the engine. The wind's getting up properly now."

If the slant of the decks was anything to go by, Helen thought they must have been bouncing around like a cork. When she tried to stand up, she felt decidedly queasy, so she sat down again quickly, and busied herself with the opening mechanism of the safe. It had rusted hard, and she couldn't even move the numbers round, but with a little oil and a lot of prodding and scraping with her knife, she managed to wrench it free. She couldn't read the numbers any longer, but she could hear the clicks as she turned the knob and reckoned that it was more or less intact.

The *Sweet Promise* groaned beneath the weight of the wind. Helen could hear Gregory yelling at Na-Tinn and a second later the engine back-fired into life. It was a strange sensation listening to the propellors fighting the swollen seas, sometimes a couple of fathoms below the surface of the waves, sometimes running free in nothing but air. The wind wrenched, buffeted and tossed them hither and thither with increasing agitation. A trickle of water came down the companionway, staining the floor and giving Helen a fright. She rushed round the cabins, making sure that all the portholes were secure, fighting her way across floors that would not lie down.

Wedged between the table and the bunk she was sitting on, Helen could just about keep her balance.

She found herself waiting for the dip and rise again of the bows, scarcely daring to breathe herself except in the same agonising rhythm. After a while she couldn't stand it any longer and thought she would go up on deck with the others, to reassure herself that she was no longer alone in this perilous world.

She was thrown backwards down the steps, but at her second attempt she gained the hatch and pulled herself up into the full terror of the storm above. Gregory was at the wheel. She could see the muscles of his arms and back bulging as they took the strain of keeping *Sweet Promise* more or less on her course. Somehow, afterwards she couldn't remember how she had done it, she crawled into the cockpit beside him and wedged herself into the small space between the wheel and the side of the boat.

"Get back below!" he roared at her.

She shook her head. "It's better up here!" she shouted into the wind.

"That's a good one!"

"No, truly! It's horrid being alone!"

He laughed and the wind caught the sound and roared its own approval. "We haven't far to go now," he comforted her.

She hung on to the edge of the rail and glanced about her, hoping to see some landmark that would be familiar. She was astonished to find that they were indeed nearly home. The harbour welcomed them with open arms, a haven of comparative peace in the middle of the howling wind. The palm trees were bent almost double and there was no sign of anyone on the Island. The flattened grass was torn out at the roots and whole clods were taken up by the wind and battered against the whining trees. It was a frightening sight.

And then it began to rain. Great drops of water fell on them from the sky, stinging their eyes and drenching them to the skin. The downpour closed in round them and they could hardly see the harbour for whirling rain and sea. Helen saw Gregory grit his teeth as he set the *Sweet Promise* to tear her way through the entrance to the harbour, holding on to the wheel with everything he had. For a moment, she thought they were crashing into the containing reef, but they rose higher and higher on the crest of some enormous wave and shot through the opening, crashing down into the furrow of the wave about fifty feet inside the lagoon. They were home.

When they came in beside the jetty, Helen saw why the Polynesians were renowned the world over for their sailing abilities. Na-Tinn tied a rope around his waist, waited for his chance and then hurled himself into space, landing in a helpless jangle of limbs on the fragile jetty. He was on his feet in a trice, putting his whole weight behind the rope to try and hold the dancing boat. When he had more or less recovered his balance, Taine-Mal followed him on to the jetty, leaping high above the breaking waves. He lost his footing on the wet bamboo, slipped between the edge of the jetty and the oncoming boat and disappeared into the boiling water. Helen's first instinct was to go to his aid, but there was nothing that she could do to help him. She stared down into the froth and grey-green water, but there was no sign of Taine-Mal's dark head. Then she saw him on the other side of the *Sweet Promise*, his head bobbing up and down. He took an enormous breath of air and dived down again into the water, reappearing alongside the jetty. He glanced round behind him, waited, tense and anxious, for the next wave to carry him right up on to the jetty. He came out of the water like a penguin rising from the sea on to a handy rock, and made fast the rope.

It was obvious that the jetty was about to break up. The wind tore at the bamboo struts and the heavy rain beat down on it with a weight it had never been designed to withstand.

"We'll have to drag the *Sweet Promise* further in," Gregory said bitterly. "Take her up the creek!"

"There isn't enough water," Helen protested.

"There is now," he retorted grimly. "Get busy battening everything down, and I'll get the lads to haul us up between those trees."

It took a long time. They secured as many lines as they could to the surrounding trees, trying not to think how easily the wind could uproot these giant palms. Gregory did what he could to protect the sides and top of the boat by covering her with a cradle of branches and leaves.

"She'll have to do," he said at last. His leg was bleeding slightly and the material of his trousers had stuck to the long line of his wound. It had been a long, long day. "Have you got the safe?" he asked Helen.

She held it up in a triumphant gesture. It was heavier than she had remembered and she could hardly stand up with the wind blowing her this way and that. She dropped to her knees and the safe landed with a thud in the mud beside her.

"I oiled the works," she gasped, trying to get her breath back, "but it still wouldn't open. You'll have to help carry it! I can't manage it alone!" She gave a despairing kick and was shocked into silence to see the door fall open and pieces of gold rushing everywhere in the mud all about her.

Gregory laughed helplessly. "You should see your face!" he shouted at her.

She smiled and picked up a handful of gold, throwing it into the wind and watching it fall several feet from her, wet and glittering. "The crock at the end of the rainbow," she exulted.

Gregory stood, ankle deep in mud, watching her. "I hope you'll always think so," he said.

## CHAPTER ELEVEN

It was hard to tell whether the rain was coming from below or above as it richocheted off the muddy ground and was blown across their path by the ever-increasing wind. Gregory took off his shirt, that was torn anyway and soaking wet, and gathered the gold pieces together, tying the sleeves round the top to hold them in. He slung it over his naked shoulder and held out a hand to Helen, helping her to her feet.

"I'll take you to the hotel," he said.

There was something in his voice that told her that he would not be staying at the hotel himself.

"Where are you going?" she asked him sharply.

"The Islanders will need help," he explained simply.

Helen turned and faced him, her feet slightly apart. "I'm going with you!" she announced with a distinct quiver in her voice.

He grinned at her. "Are you any good at keeping children quiet?" he asked her.

She would have said anything not to have been left behind. She was prepared to put up with anything at all rather than be left waiting and worrying about him at the hotel.

"I won't go to the hotel on my own," she said mutinously.

"I must be mad!" was all Gregory said. "We'd better drop off the gold there anyway. Afterwards, we'll need to gather all the villagers together at some central point."

Helen shivered. "Those houses can't be much protection against this kind of storm. Why don't they build something more solid?"

"They bend. Anything more solid might break. Look, will you wait here while I go to the hotel?"

But she was too scared to wait anywhere on her own. She clung to his hand, following in his footsteps, until she saw the lights of the hotel only a few feet in front of her. She was mildly surprised that the electricity should still have been working, but there it was, a great wall of light in the grey, gloomy surroundings.

The wind had shattered the glass in the French windows round the back. Gregory released one of the catches and the door flew open, dragging them into the room beyond and slamming against the wall. A dozen people flew to the gaping entrance and forced the door shut again.

"My, you poor things!" a sympathetic woman said to them. "I'll tell them in the office that you're back."

Helen felt self-conscious as she stood, dripping on to the clean floor, uncomfortably aware of the muddy spectacle she must present. She was relieved when Anita came running over to her, slipping warm, dry arms about her, and whispering: "Darling, I thought the wind would sink you! It was awful! Can you hear it against the building? It shakes so! Peter says it's silly to be afraid, but I can't help it!"

"You're all right here," Helen soothed her. "Miss Corrigan will soon tell you if there's any danger."

Anita laughed hysterically. "That old woman! She's busy reading a thriller and doesn't want to be disturbed!"

Gregory's laughter burst out across the room. "I'll soon disturb her!" he threatened. "She's needed in the village! Who does she think is going to bandage all the broken limbs and sing to the children?"

Helen found herself laughing too. "I thought I was," she smiled.

He grinned at her. "The more the merrier. Ethel

can speak to them in their own language. I'll go and winkle her out! Get Peter to put this in the hotel safe, will you?"

There was a gasp from the American guests that could be heard above the wind when they saw the gold pieces glinting through the frayed cloth of Gregory's shirt. They all wanted to look at them, to see what they were like.

"Did you really get them back from the sea?" they asked Helen breathlessly.

She was embarrassed. "Gregory did," she said.

Their intrigued glances followed Gregory into the foyer. With his bare feet and naked torso, he looked like one of the Islanders himself. His dark hair glistened black from the rain, and water ran in rivulets down his chest and on to the deep, luxurious carpets with which he formed such a contrast.

"He looks the part!" Anita giggled.

"What do you mean?" Helen shot at her.

"I don't know," the other girl shrugged. "You know! He looks like a pirate without any shirt—or anything!"

"Nonsense!" Helen said sharply.

"But he does!" Anita giggled again. "I hadn't noticed before, but he does!"

But Helen refused to look at him again. When she did, her heart shook within her, and she felt more uncomfortable than ever. If he looked like that, what on earth must she be looking like? She put up a hand to her dripping hair and tried to wring out some of the excess water.

"You'd better go and change," Anita said frankly. "I'll mix you a drink while you're gone."

"But they might go without me!" Helen objected.

"So what?" her sister-in-law retorted.

"I have to go," Helen said. "It's important—"

Anita sighed. "Well, if you must, you must," she said. "But you look absolutely ghastly now, if you want to know! I shouldn't have thought a change of clothes would have hurt!"

"Will you keep the drinks till I get back?" Helen pleaded with her.

Anita smiled an odd, lop-sided smile. "I will," she promised. "And I'll give your gold to Peter to look after, if you can bear to part with it. It'll be quite safe with him!"

Helen thanked her and hurried into the lift. Now that she had been goaded into it, she had to admit that she would be pleased to change into dry clothes and wash the worst of the mud off her hands and feet. Even so, she was unprepared for the sight of herself in the looking glass. Muddy splotches covered her face and her hair hung down like string all round her neck. Her clothes were badly torn, and she had lost a button from the front of her shirt that gave her a decidedly rakish air.

"Good heavens!" she said to herself, and then again, "Good heavens!"

She stripped off her clothes as fast as she could and dried herself on one of the hotel towels, hoping that Peter wouldn't be too shocked at the sad spectacle it presented when she had finished with it. She felt decidedly better when she was both clean and dry. She could even laugh at herself, for when she had first seen herself in the glass, she had wondered what Gregory must have thought of her. What should he have thought? She was nothing to him, just as he was nothing to her!

She pulled on a clean pair of jeans and a polo-necked sweater and brushed her hair until it stood up in a halo all round her head. Then with a comb, she restored it ruthlessly to order, and looked at herself with satisfaction. Without any make-up on, she looked younger than she really was, but otherwise she was as neat and as unremarkable as the most self-effacing widow could wish to be. Perhaps it was that that made her choose her brightest lipstick and, with a defiant gesture, apply it freely to her pale lips.

The electricity went off just as she was leaving her room. The whole building shook and was plunged into darkness. Helen could hear a female scream reverberating through the hotel and hoped that it wasn't Anita. Then there was complete silence and, a few seconds later, Peter's voice, demanding that someone should light the candles to give the guests some kind of light.

Helen crept along the corridor, playing blind man's buff with the wall as she searched for the head of the stairs. It was a long way down, but at least she knew where she was going. When she reached the bottom, she could see the flickering candles in the foyer, and looked about hastily for Gregory.

At first she thought he wasn't there, but he came over to her immediately and pressed a drink into her hand.

"It'll keep your spirits up," he told her cheerfully.

She took a sip, gasped, and took another. She had no idea what was in it, but it tasted good. "Did you find Miss Corrigan?" she asked.

"I did!" he said.

"Spoiling a perfectly good afternoon," the old lady complained. "I always have a rest after my lunch. You should know that by now!"

"We don't always have a typhoon to contend with," he reminded her patiently.

Miss Corrigan listened to the wind. "It's got some way to go yet," she snorted. "Experience has taught me not to anticipate trouble, young man! But as you quite obviously won't give me any peace, I'm ready when you are!"

Gregory grinned. "Helen is coming too," he told her. "She wants to help—"

"If I can," Helen put in humbly.

"Glad to have you," Miss Corrigan said emphatically. "The Islanders like you! Just as they like this young man of yours!"

Helen could feel herself blushing. The colour rolled up her cheeks and she felt weak at the knees. "It's this drink," she exclaimed. "It's going to my head!"

Miss Corrigan looked at her in astonishment. "Nonsense, my dear!" she said briskly. "You won't be any use to any of us if you're drunk!"

"How very true!" Gregory agreed in an amused voice. He took the drink from her and handed it to Anita. "There's no knowing what she might do!" he added conspiratorially.

Anita was put out. "But Helen *never*—" she began.

"You mean she hasn't yet!" Gregory corrected her gravely.

"And just what are you implying?" Helen stormed at him. She worked herself into a fine rage, for she found it very much easier to be angry than the other curious feeling, tinged with failure and embarrassment, that seemed to have dogged her all day.

"That there are a lot of things you've never done before, what else?" Gregory teased her.

"Like what?" she demanded.

He chuckled. "One of these days I'll tell you exactly," he said. "But right now, I think we ought to be going."

The look on Anita's face pleaded with her not to go. "Stay here with us," she begged. "The hotel must be safer than the village. Oh, Helen, I couldn't bear it if anything happened to you!"

"Nothing will," Helen assured her comfortably. "Don't worry, darling. Peter will look after you!"

Anita's face cleared as if by magic. "Yes, he will, won't he?" she said on a note of relief. "But I'm sure he'd look after you too!" She looked scornfully at Gregory. "*He* probably won't have time!"

Helen grinned. "I thought you said he was never beastly?" she laughed.

But Anita was not amused. "I've changed my mind," she said primly. "He expects too much!"

Helen swallowed. She had the uncomfortable sensation that she was getting out of her depth again. Her eyes met Gregory's and she saw that his were full of laughter.

"Do I expect too much?" he asked her.

She shook her head, not knowing what any of them were talking about. "I don't know," she said foolishly, and wondered why he laughed.

Peter had busied himself lighting half a dozen storm lamps for them to take with them. It wasn't quite dark, but the storm had brought the evening early and the light was a comfort to them all.

"Mrs. Hastings," he said dryly, as he handed one of the lamps to Helen. "Don't get lost!" he added.

And that summed it all up, she thought. She would be Mrs. Hastings till she died.


The trees were black and gaunt against the rain-washed, grey sky. Stripped of their leaves by the wind, what was left of them rattled and fought for survival against the driving rain. The wind moaned over the island like an evil presence. There was no place to hide from it, as it tore at one's clothing and one's hair. It was hard work to make any way against it, and no matter which way one turned, there it was, still blowing into one's face.

Helen struggled down the track after Gregory, glad of his solid presence in front of her. Behind her came Miss Corrigan, grumbling and weary, but game to the last.

"The village looks deserted to me," Helen shrieked through the wind, as they approached the grass-built huts where most of the people lived.

"They're in the long hut," Miss Corrigan panted back. "They'll all be together at a time like this!"

Gregory glanced impatiently behind him. He gave a tug to Helen's sleeve to signal to her to hurry up, but there was no hurrying Miss Corrigan. The old lady was struggling along as best she could, but with the rain in her face and the wind pulling at her bulky figure, it was as much as she could do to make any progress at all.

"Come on!" Gregory yelled at them.

Helen linked her arm round the old lady's and hauled her along the path. It was like walking through a river, so much rain had fallen and had been unable to get away. The water rushed over their ankles, dragging at their feet and pulling them off balance. Even Gregory was having difficulty. He favoured his bad leg as much as he could, wincing away from every step, but he wanted to get them there before the typhoon came to a head, and that meant racing against time all the way.

The long hut was crowded with shivering people. There was complete silence in the long, wide room, apart from the wind beating against the fragile structure and the plaited grass of the sides slapping against the poles to which they were fixed. No one spoke. The children huddled together in fright, and the adults were almost as bad. Most of them had sunk into the silence of despair. They sat and waited for the typhoon to pass over them, shutting their ears with their hands, and moaning to themselves in competition with the wind.

Helen held her lamp high so that they could see where they were stepping and pushed Miss Corrigan through the entrance in front of her. The old lady looked round the room, completely calm and in possession of herself. "My, my, it looks like a funeral!" she said. "This will never do!"

One or two of the children came running across to her and she spoke to them softly in their own tongue, laughing at their frightened faces. Helen, too, pushed her way further into the room and found herself in the centre of a clutch of children who held on to her with tight little hands, seeking comfort from anyone who could give it to them.

Helen did her best to reassure them. She hung the lights all down down the centre of the room, talking to them as she did so. Even that small gesture seemed to make them feel better, she noticed. They gathered round Miss Corrigan in increasing numbers, while the old lady, wet to the skin and looking like a large, fat, half-drowned rat, began to tell them stories of the exploits of their ancestors. She told them of the first Polynesian sailors, who had sailed across the Pacific on boats that were little better than rafts, with only a star to guide them. She told them of how they had spread through the islands. Of how they had reached Hawaii, and Fiji, and Tonga; of how the Maoris had travelled to New Zealand, the land of the long white cloud; and how their own fore-fathers had come to the Islands of Melonga and had settled there.

Helen found herself listening to the stories too. Some of them she found hard to understand, but others were familiar to her and she could fill in the details for herself when she couldn't understand the strange words that Miss Corrigan used to describe their customs and the dug-out canoes they still sailed from one island to the other in the Melonga group.

In the middle of one of these tales, Helen was horrified to observe that one of the women was weeping. She knelt down beside her, surprised as she always was when she was near to any member of the Polynesian race by the sheer size of the magnificent bronzed body that rose from the floor in a mountain of solid, ample flesh. She put her arms about the woman's massive shape and hugged her, but the woman wept on.

"What's the matter?" she asked her.

"The children," the woman gasped.

"What about the children?" Helen asked her. But the woman would say no more.

"Having trouble?" Gregory whispered. Helen nodded. She pointed to the woman and explained what she had said.

"Perhaps she means her children," he hazarded. "I'll ask her." He knelt down beside her on the floor, holding his hand tightly over his thigh to ease the pressure on his found. He was as gentle as Helen had ever seen him and her eyes misted over with tears as she watched him console the tearful creature between them, speaking to her in the pidgin English that all the Islanders understood as well as they did their own tongue.

"She's lost her children," he said to Helen, when he had finally got the story out of her. "Her husband insisted that she should come to the long hut alone. He's still outside looking for the youngsters and she fears for their lives."

"Where were they when she last saw them?" Helen asked.

"On the other side of the island. They'd gone to look at the place where the shark was killed."

"Alone?" Helen was appalled by the thought. She knew the difficulty they had had in coming the short way from the hotel. How could small children find their way right across the island alone?

"What are we going to do?" she murmured.

"There's only one thing we can do," Gregory said in a voice that was drained of all emotion. "I shall have to go out and look for them. At least I should run into their father somewhere along the route."

"But you can't!"

"I must," he replied more gently still. "You don't understand. When the eye of the typhoon passes over, who knows what it might bring with it? There may be a tidal wave that will completely submerge a small beach like that. And if it goes directly over us, there won't be much left in its path."

"But why does it have to be you?" she pleaded.

His eyes were as dark and as enigmatic as ever. "Would you rather that I left them to their fate?" he asked.

She shook her head and turned away from him. She hadn't much left, but at least she had enough pride not to show him how frightened she was. She wouldn't even look up when he stood up and tightened his leather belt round his waist. And it was too late when she turned to tell him that, after all, she knew he had to go. Gregory had already slipped out through the grass-plaited wall and was gone.

They were left in no doubt when the centre of the typhoon passed over. There was a minute's breathless hush, when the wind dropped to a murmur and the rain ceased as abruptly as it had started. In the long hut, the chatter that Miss Corrigan had so ably encouraged muted to a startled intake of breath and ceased altogether. The waiting seemed endless.

"Pray heaven Gregory has found those children!" Miss Corrigan said. "This is what I meant when I said it would get worse!"

It was like an agony to listen and to hear nothing. Then like a roar, they heard it coming. First they could hear the churning sea, whirling into a circular pillar of water, dust and cloud, that hit the land with such a force that the whole island trembled. There was the sound of rushing water, which came so close that Helen thought it must go right over them. It reached the outskirts of the village and swept away some of the huts, before it roared out to sea again.

But if the tidal wave was to do damage, it was nothing like that wrought by the whirlwind as it circled round the island like some crazy giant, uprooting trees and tossing whole buildings from one end of the island to the other. Nothing could escape its fury. Roofs were torn off the Government buildings and corrugated iron whirled hundreds of feet into the air, to come crashing down many miles away, if it were ever to reappear at all. The whole island was shattered, trampled on, and the cultivated land ruined by the salt from the sea.

Then, as suddenly as it had ceased, the rain poured down again and the wind buffeted against what remained as angrily as ever.

"Is it safe to go out now?" Helen asked.

Miss Corrigan nodded. "But I doubt you'll find him," she said. "You'd do better to wait here for him to come back to us. He'll come, never fear. Gregory de Vaux is not the type to allow himself to be washed away."

"But his leg was hurting him!" Helen burst out. "It had started bleeding again! Didn't you notice?"

"I noticed. I didn't figure it would help to remark on it!"

Helen stood helplessly looking out at the stricken night. "You don't understand—" she began.

"My dear girl, it's as plain as the nose on your face!" Miss Corrigan contradicted her. "You've fallen in love with the man and you can't bear to be apart from him! Well, that's natural enough! But you'd do better to wait for him here all the same."

Helen was shocked. "But that isn't right!"

Miss Corrigan's dewlap quivered. "What isn't right?"

"I've been in love," Helen said faintly. "I'm not in love with Gregory."

"Then I'd like to know what you call it!" the old lady snorted.

Helen stared at her. "I work for him," she said. "And he doesn't like women anyway. Right from the start I've had to be better than anyone else he could get, or he would have sacked me on the spot—"

"And who told you he didn't like women?" Miss Corrigan demanded crossly. "He likes me well enough!"

"That isn't what I meant," Helen said uncomfortably.

"That's obvious!" Miss Corrigan agreed. "My, but your father would have been ashamed that any daughter of his would turn out to be so stupid, half-baked— yes, *adolescent*, Helen MacNeil!"

"I'm not a MacNeil any longer," Helen said flatly. "I'm Helen Hastings now!"

"And much good it's done you! When you came here, at least you were honest enough to admit that you didn't know whether you had been in love with Michael Hastings. It's odd that you seem to have become more and more sure of it!"

Aware that the islanders were watching the irate old lady with open mouths, Helen swallowed her own anger, contenting herself with glaring out into the darkness. She would go back to teaching and never go diving again. Teaching was a nice, safe profession where one met nobody but eager children, who might be dull, but who didn't expect more from their teacher than she was prepared to give.

"I'm not sure," she said. "I'm not sure of anything!"

"Then you'd better get the children engaged in some game until you are sure!" Miss Corrigan told her tartly. She was rewarded by a rather limp smile and patted Helen hard on her arm. "Just don't go on mooning about Michael Hastings. He isn't worth it dead and he wasn't worth it alive. Whatever Anita might think!" she added crushingly.

It was morning before the wind dropped. The dawn flooded over the Pacific Ocean in a haze of colour. Clouds, that had been dark and threatening the night

175

before, were now no more than pink, apricot and yellow fluffs of cotton wool. Only the long trails of vapour across the horizon gave evidence to the trail of the typhoon which had passed that way. The sea was a strong royal blue, capped with dancing crowns of white, which had nothing in common with the tidal wave that had swept across the island the night before.

It was a second or two before Helen could remember where she was. The sun crept across the floor, casting peculiar patterns of shade as it came in through the plaited walls. Everything in the long hut was damp and steaming and the people presented a sorry sight. Dirty puddles had gathered on the mats on the floor and the children had lain in them and were all of them muddy, tired and fractious. The grown-ups sat in silence, awed by the relief that gripped them that it was all over and that they, at least, had escaped the fury of the storm comparatively unscathed. A dog, who taken shelter unnoticed with his young master, barked loudly, his tail wagging ferociously with sheer joy of living. Somewhere else, a woman hugged her children to her, chiding them for the mess they had got themselves into.

Helen forced herself upright and yawned. Miss Corrigan was still asleep. Her mouth had fallen open and her clothes were wet and sadly crumpled. Helen covered her with a blanket, feeling a rush of tenderness for her. How old was she, to walk uncomplainingly through the storm to bring comfort to a few of her islanders? She would be stiff and uncomfortable for days after this and yet she had probably thought it all worth it. But Helen herself couldn't stay in the hut any longer. She stretched her arms and legs and was pleased to find that she wasn't stiff at all. She wasn't even tired any longer.

Outside, the sun was already warm, but the smell of the fresh air was the best part of the morning. She filled her lungs with it, while she looked around the village, to see what was left and what could be rebuilt. And then she saw him. Gregory came down the track towards her, followed by three small children. A few feet behind the children came their father, proud and smiling, but Helen hardly saw him at all. It was enough for her to know that Gregory was safe.

"Where were you?" she cried, wiping the sudden tears from her cheeks.

He grinned at her. "We managed," he said. "How about you?"

# CHAPTER TWELVE

"WHAT are you going to do now that it's all over?" Anita asked Helen.

She prowled restlessly round the room, touching this and that as she went, never quite looking in Helen's direction.

"I'm going back to teaching," Helen told her.

"In England?" Anita shot at her.

Helen shrugged her shoulders. "I really don't know." She sighed. "I might try New Zealand—at least your mother isn't likely to come out and visit me there!"

To her dismay, Anita began to cry. She hunched up her shoulders and allowed the tears to pour down her cheeks, ruining her make-up and somehow destroying all of her new-found confidence and sophistication.

"But what am I to do?" she wailed.

Helen took her by the hand and pulled her to the window. "Look down there," she said. "Look at the swimming pool and the grounds of the hotel. Isn't that what you want? Why don't you stay on here?"

"I want *Peter!*" Anita cried the harder.

"Then why don't you go down and see if he wants you?" Helen suggested encouragingly. "You could ask him for a job here for a start and see what he says, couldn't you?"

Anita sniffed. "D'you think he'll *mind*?"

Helen smiled at her. "No, I don't think he'll mind," she said. She smothered her mild feeling of irritation with her sister-in-law and made her wash her face and put on some fresh make-up. "Why don't you go now?" she suggested.

When Anita had gone, she finished her own toilet. The electricity had been fixed immediately after breakfast, and so she had made an appointment with the hotel's as yet untried hairdressing establishment, though what they were going to be able to do for her, she didn't quite know. Her hair had been in and out of salt water too often recently to look its best, and the storm of the night before had just about finished it off.

The Spanish-American hairdresser, however, refused to be depressed. With scarcely a word of English, he cut and washed and finally set her hair in a style of his own improvisation, but which he assured her she would like. To Helen, it didn't seem to matter very much. She allowed herself to be ushered from seat to seat, and did her best to follow one of the stories in a glossy American magazine, but even that couldn't hold her interest. After the typhoon, and now that the gold was safe, nothing seemed to matter very much.

She heard a slight commotion in the main body of the salon, but with the noise of the drier in her ears, she couldn't hear what it was all about, so she turned her attention back to her magazine. She was quite unprepared therefore for Peter's angry appearance directly in front of her. He mouthed something at her, his face white with temper, and she ducked her head out of the drier to hear what he had to say.

"What?" she said to him.

"What have you done to Anita?" he shouted at her.

"*Anita?*"

He slapped his hands down on the arms of her chair, making her a prisoner with the roaring drier just behind her.

"Yes, Anita. What have you been saying to her. Why did you have to upset her?"

"I wasn't aware that I had," Helen began.

"Oh, come now! You can't expect me to believe that! Dragging her back to England because you want to go! Doesn't it ever occur to you to consider anyone else's feeling but your own?"

"Well, yes, it does, as a matter of fact," Helen retorted. She had an uncomfortable urge to laugh, but she knew that Peter was in no mood for levity. "Perhaps, if you told me what's wrong—"

"You won't get away with it! I suspected from the beginning that you didn't *like* Anita, but to do this to her— It's too much!"

"So I see," Helen said gently.

Peter looked slightly embarrassed. "I don't mean you weren't kind bringing her out here in the first place—"

"I wanted to," Helen reminded him.

"Yes, well, that was kind," he agreed. "But why make her go home now?"

Helen began to wonder exactly what Anita could have said to him. "I wasn't aware," she said lightly, "that I was making her do anything."

Peter stared straight at her. He looked very young and eager, and more bewildered now than angry. "Helen, tell the truth!" he pleaded with her. "Would Anita stay on here with me?"

"I should ask her," Helen said.

"You won't stop her?"

"I wouldn't want to try," she assured him.

He stood up straight, looking more puzzled than ever. "I can't understand it," he said. "Why should she want me to believe that you were going to take her away to England?"

Helen smiled. "Perhaps she wanted to see if you would stop her?" she suggested.

To her amusement, Peter's white face went quite pink. "Oh, do you think so?" he asked her, mightily pleased.

"I do," Helen laughed. "But I think I should warn you that your future mother-in-law is something more than a music-hall joke. I know, believe me!"

He grinned, momentarily amused. "She won't bother me," he declared. "America won the last War of Independence and I intend to see that she wins this one too if necessary!"

Helen could only admire his attitude. "Good for you!" she said. She hoped he would win, but her own experience with her mother-in-law had made her rather bitter on the subject and she knew it.

Peter kissed her lightly on the cheek and put up a teasing hand to feel if her hair were dry. "Another few minutes," he said professionally. "But you'd better hurry it up," he added as an afterthought. "Gregory is looking for you!"

Helen sank back under the drier, aghast at the awful apathy that grasped her. Only one thought kept hammering at her sheer reluctance to do anything in case she ran into Gregory. She had to keep away from him. She would find it quite pleasant to go to New Zealand and find herself a job there. She would grow to like teaching again, she knew she would. But not if she had to argue every inch of the way with Gregory first. They would go round and round in circles, making themselves more and more miserable, when all the time she knew perfectly well what had to be done.

She had fallen in love and she had married Michael Hastings. It was too late now to regret that fact. It had happened. And, because it had happened, it meant that what she felt whenever Gregory came near her was not love at all! Why, she had loved Michael, hadn't she? She had worried about him, and she had liked him, and she would have gone on liking him. She certainly hadn't wanted to kiss him at one moment and hit him the next. She hadn't hated him so much that she had been spent with sheer agony of the emotion. Nor had she wanted his attention, his *exclusive* attention, in spite of disliking him. She hadn't cried all over him at the slightest excuse, but then she hadn't laughed much either. And that had been love? It must have been love, she told herself desperately. People like her didn't marry the Michaels of this world for no reason at all—did they?

By the time the hairdresser had released her from the drier, and had combed out her hair to his satisfaction amidst a shower of Spanish superlatives as to how perfectly it had turned out, Helen was thoroughly frightened. She hurried away from the salon to her room and did her best to restore some kind of order amongst her emotions. Life, she told herself grimly, had to go on. And she wasn't helping things, or herself, to go on like this, scared as a rabbit and twice as silly!

The telephone rang. Helen forced herself to answer it with a quiet "Yes" that gave nothing away.

"It's Anita!" a female squeal told her. "Peter and I are going to get married! And, Helen, Gregory wants you—*now*!"

"You'd better come," Anita said quickly. "I think he'll come and get you otherwise!"

Helen slammed down the receiver. She would have to go, she supposed, but she was not pleased at being summoned in such a cavalier way. Even so she couldn't help noticing that she did look nice. She caught a glimpse of herself in the looking glass as she walked across the room, smart, even a little sophisticated, and looking faintly unfamiliar in a tailored coat and skirt. She only hoped she could find a manner to match when she told Gregory that she was leaving just as soon as she could lay on the pilot to take her out of the Islands and back to New Zealand.

It seemed as though everyone had gathered in the

foyer downstairs. Peter was busily opening bottles of Californian champagne to celebrate his engagement to Anita and everyone else had gathered round to join in the general excitement. At first, Helen didn't see Gregory. She was busy congratulating Anita, suddenly overwhelmingly glad at her sister-in-law's happiness.

"Don't let anything spoil it for you," she whispered to her.

"I won't!" Anita assured her. "I won't even tell her until after the ceremony."

It was then that Helen saw Gregory. He looked straight at her and her stomach turned over within her.

"I thought we had a contract?" he drawled over the top of his champagne glass.

"But it's finished," she said. There was an annoying catch to her voice that she hoped he hadn't noticed.

"Has it?"

"Well, we—we brought up the gold," she said.

He went on looking at her. "I see," he said. "So it's glory for the female crew after all, and the hard work for the men!"

"That isn't fair!" she protested. "I've worked as hard as anyone!"

"But you're quite prepared to leave your equipment in a mess, the *Sweet Promise* abandoned halfway up a creek and in need of a coat of paint, and your week's money only half earned!"

She didn't know what to say to that. She hadn't thought about it at all. All she had known was that he wouldn't need her any more.

"You hired me as a diver," she said mutinously, "not as a maintenance man!"

"I took you on to the strength of the expedition," he replied smoothly. "And that means turning your hand to anything, *anything at all*, Helen Hastings, until the expedition is finished. Is that clear?"

She nodded meekly. It wasn't nearly as easy to tell him that she was going as she had thought it would be.

"Besides," Gregory added bitingly, "what *diver* would leave her equipment like that? Did you think I was going to put it away for you? What you want is a nanny, not a boss!"

"I'm sorry," she muttered. This wasn't going at all the way she had imagined.

He grunted. "I'll expect you after lunch," he said. "And you'd better come dressed for it! Those things don't look very practical for our kind of work!"

It was, however, a lunch to remember. Gregory made a clever and rather witty speech that had everyone howling with laughter, and the only person who felt at all left out was Helen. It was so unfair, she thought, for she had worked hard, and Anita hadn't done a thing to earn her money, and yet he had nothing but praise for her sister-in-law, while her he didn't even mention. She might just as well not have worked for him at all!

"The gold," he added amidst applause, "has been handed over to the Government. The wealth of the islands has been restored to them. We all of us will be starting out on new adventures, but the Melonga Islands, and the memories of our days here, will be a link between us for the rest of our days."

Helen could have wept. She didn't want to remember. She wanted to forget! And she would forget, she promised herself, she would forget every moment she had spent there—

Then it was all over and everybody was busy chatting. She would have to go upstairs and change, she supposed, for she didn't dare keep Gregory waiting. He was right in a way, she admitted to herself, for the equipment would have to be stowed away before she could consider her job really finished. What she couldn't excuse was the public way he had pointed it out to her.

She found herself hurrying though as she went down the path, through the devastated village, and on to the empty harbour. From there, she could see the *Sweet Promise* towering over the creek where they had left her. She was well and truly grounded, listing terribly over the muddy bank that was helping to support her. Gregory must have been there that morning and removed most of the debris from her decks, but even so she looked a sad and sorry sight. Her white paint had blistered and rusted, her sails hung in torn confusion, and a bewildering pile of abandoned diving equipment littered her foredecks in a manner that was anything but shipshape.

Helen swung herself on board and looked helplessly about her. It was hard to know where to begin. She tossed a few empty cylinders ashore, to make a little more room, and then set to with a will, washing everything that came within reach and stowing everything else away where it belonged.

She must have been working for about an hour when Gregory arrived. He swung himself up on board and stood on the sloping deck, watching her work.

"I'm afraid the sails have had it," he said finally.

"We might be able to patch them," Helen suggested eagerly.

"*We*?" he asked.

She blushed. "It was a manner of speaking," she said abruptly. "What I mean is that I think it could be done!"

"I dare say," he agreed, and smiled like a small boy. "But we're in the money now. It's the first time I've been able to afford to do something for the old lady. I think she deserves new sails, don't you?"

She sat back on her heels and looked up at the tall

masts and thought of the way she had come through
the storm and brought them safely home to harbour.

"Yes, she deserves everything you can give her," she
agreed softly.

"I'm glad you agree," Gregory went on briskly. "Anita
was in no state to do much about anything, so I put in
an order for some paint myself. They're flying it out on
the next flight."

"Oh?" Helen said cautiously.

"Mmm. Having got her stuck in the creek, it makes
a pretty good dry dock, doesn't it? I thought I'd get
her painted before we haul her back down into the
harbour."

"But you'll never manage it alone!" Helen exclaimed.

"There's Na-Tinn and Taine-Mal," he pointed out.

"And have either of them ever painted a boat
before?" she demanded.

"There has to be a first time!"

Helen turned her back on him and went on tidying
away the ropes that were strewn across the deck.
Another moment and she would have offered to have
stayed. She had no pride at all!

"Shall I make some coffee?" she said, when the
silence became unbearable.

"I thought we'd run out," he answered.

"We have," she admitted helplessly. "Oh well, it was
just an idea!"

She wished he would do anything, anything at all,
but stand there, watching her every movement.

"I'm not going to offer to stay!" she burst out
furiously at last.

"What did you say?" he asked with friendly interest.

She turned and faced him. "You heard!" she said
angrily. "Haven't you anything to do?"

"I expect I could find something," he agreed, grinning. "I was enjoying the view."

"So I gather! Well, you made your point back at the

hotel. I agree with you! I should have seen that everything was shipshape before I started to think about leaving. Not that you had to tell the whole hotel about it!" she added, for she was still smarting under his rebuke. "I would have come anyway. But then to sit there and watch me is just too much!"

Gregory began to laugh. "I didn't know you cared!" he teased her.

"I don't," she snapped. "But surely there is *something* you can do besides check up on me?"

"Is that what I'm doing?" he said mildly. "How odd, I thought I was resting my leg, which incidentally is hurting quite a lot, and having an easy day after an appalling night that I want to forget all about, with children scared half to death, and me worrying myself about you!"

Helen blinked. "You've made me feel a cad now," she said.

"I'm sorry," he said. "I didn't mean to do that. Shall I go up to the hotel and get some coffee?"

She nodded, not trusting herself to speak. She waited until he had jumped down on to the bank below and then she called after him: "I'm coming too! Wait for me!"

She was in such a hurry that she didn't notice that she had left one of the lines across her path and, instead of jumping, she half fell, landing practically on top of Gregory below. He opened his arms wide to receive her, taking the full impact of her fall against his own body.

"I—I'm sorry!" she gasped.

Gregory laughed. "My love, do you have to take everything so seriously? Didn't you know that I've been waiting all day for you to fall into my arms?"

Helen stiffened. "L—literally?" she stammered, before she had thought.

"I'd have preferred a more voluntary means of propulsion," he said with humour, then let her go with a sigh. "We're not making much progress, are we?" he added.

Helen forced a laugh. "I don't know. I've practically finished with the diving tackle!" she said brightly.

His hands came down on her shoulders, and they weren't a bit gentle. Slowly, ruthlessly, he turned her round to face him. "In just a minute," he said, "I'm going to kiss you. And then I'm going to kiss you again. And I'm going on kissing you until you admit that you like it—"

"I—I'll never speak to you again!" she threatened, badly frightened.

"Won't you?" There was a touch of grimness about his mouth that made her tremble.

"You don't understand—" she began helplessly.

"I think I do," he answered. "I wish I didn't."

She sat down heavily on the bank of the creek, because her legs refused point blank to carry her any longer. "You see," she said quickly, "I'm not a young girl who—who—" She broke off, not knowing how to continue. She wished he wasn't so tall, towering above her like some giant, and she wished he wouldn't smile at her.

"You look pretty young to me!" he remarked.

"Yes, but—"

"But there was Michael!" Gregory sighed.

She looked up at him mutinously. "Yes," she said, "there was Michael."

He went on standing there, not really looking at her at all. His eyes wandered over the *Sweet Promise* and he half-frowned at the sight she presented. "You know," he said at last, "when I first met Michael, I felt sorry for him. I used to wonder what kind of a woman it was that he had married, that she wasn't right there beside him, sharing things with him." He saw she was about to protest and silenced her with a gesture. "That was at first," he said. "Then I tried to get to know him better, but there wasn't anyone there to know. He had charm and good looks and, for all I knew, a nice family who worried about him. And he had a wife."

"It was your fault I wasn't here with him!" Helen informed him. "It was *you* who wouldn't have any women around!"

"That wasn't strictly true," he contradicted her. "I wouldn't employ a married diver on a job like this—"

"But Michael *was* married!"

"He didn't look very married to me," Gregory observed. "I thought at first it was your fault, but it wasn't, was it? It was his. He shouldn't have married anyone. He didn't know what it was all about!"

Helen studied her hands. "Nevertheless, I married him," she sighed.

Gregory squatted down beside her. "You know what Miss Corrigan says it was?" he asked her. "Calf love! You weren't married, my love! You may have gone through a ceremony and thought yourself in love with him, but if that's your idea of marriage, it isn't mine!"

"You make it sound so *cheap*," she said.

He put his arm round her. "Do I? I don't mean to. I'm just trying to point out that it was a charming idyll, not a marriage!" He looked at her anxiously and was surprised to discover that she was smiling.

"And that it's over?" she suggested audaciously.

"Yes, I suppose so." He sounded almost apologetic. "It is, isn't it?" he almost pleaded with her.

She nodded. "It never really began," she admitted.

She was ready for him when he kissed her. She allowed herself to be pushed back against the muddy grass and she welcomed the sheer, solid strength of his body against hers. He smelt nice too, she thought. He smelt so masculine and different from herself. And then he kissed her gently on the lips, almost as if he were afraid of her. But the next kiss was decidedly better. She put up her arms and held him closer, and he wasn't gentle at all.

She was shaking when he released her. She sat up

quickly and brushed the hair out of her eyes. Gregory looked mightily pleased with himself and, she thought, he had something to be pleased about. If he had wanted to prove his point to her, he had certainly succeeded!

"I think we'd better go and get the coffee," she said hastily.

He grinned at her. "Not until you've said it," he answered, shaking his head.

"Said what? Oh, *that*!" She chuckled. "Why should I?" she added recklessly. But then she could afford to be generous, she thought, as she caught a glimpse of the faint uncertainty that was still in his eyes. "I love you, Gregory de Vaux," she said. "I love you more than I can say, more than life itself."

He was startled and then more pleased and flattered than she could have thought possible. "Oh, my dear!" he said brokenly, "that's more than I deserve. I thought perhaps you were attracted, and that attraction might carry us until I could make you love me—"

This time it was she who kissed him, kissing away the words that were so lacking in his usual self-confidence. "You did make me love you," she told him in a whisper. "Only I was too stupid to see it was love. All I knew was that I wanted to be with you. You—you weren't very gentle, were you?"

"I didn't feel gentle!" he retorted. "I could have wrung your neck for being so obtuse!"

She chuckled. "I'm surprised you didn't," she said comfortably.

He kissed her again. "Woman," he said, "it may surprise you, but your time may come! Waiting for something I want doesn't come easily to me!"

She ducked out of his restraining arms and stood up. "No," she said thoughtfully, "I can see it doesn't. But you will wait, won't you? It's going to be too lovely a thing to be together to have any regrets about anything." She bit her lip anxiously. "Do you mind?"

He stood up too. "Darling, I do love you!" he said.

The afternoon was almost over when they had finished working on the *Sweet Promise*.

"Will you brew up some more coffee?" Gregory called down to her through the hatch. "I've done about all I'm going to up here!"

Helen laughed. She knew it was no more than an excuse for him to come and join her in the saloon, but she went and made the coffee all the same. She liked to watch him, as much as he did her, and though she protested several times during the afternoon that they would never get the *Sweet Promise* ready to put to sea again at the rate they were going, it was just talk, for they had all the time in the world ahead of them.

"What are you going to do now?" she asked as Gregory unpinned the plan of the sunken frigate and put it away in a drawer.

"*We* are going for a trip through the Islands," he answered. "When we get tired of that, I might buy a lagoon and farm green turtles for a living. Would you like that?"

"Could you?" she said.

"Why not? If I net over one of their breeding beaches, I'd get thousands in a single season. It's the birds that get them all as the newly hatched turtles run for the sea. It should be a very paying proposition. Besides," he added, "I like turtles!"

She nodded. She didn't care much what they did as long as they did it together. "Did you hear something?" she asked him suddenly.

"Do I smell coffee?" Miss Corrigan's voice shouted up to them from the bank. "May I come aboard?"

It took the two of them to heave her up the side and to help her across the sloping deck and down below. Miss Corrigan sat down thankfully in the saloon and smiled at them both with real pleasure.

"I wanted to thank you," she said earnestly, "for

your help with the islanders last night. In fact, we all want to thank you. Just as soon as we've cleared up a bit, we'll have a party." She looked at them more closely. "I'd say you'd better get married at the same time," she added dryly.

Gregory and Helen exchanged amused glances. "We intend to!" they said.

Miss Corrigan's dewlap quivered wildly. "Well, that's a mercy!" she said fiercely. "Now, where's that coffee?"